Eminently
Respectable
CAPERS

TONY BRENNAN

ISBN: 978-1-925590-76-0
Published by Vivid Publishing
P.O. Box 948, Fremantle
Western Australia 6959
www.vividpublishing.com.au

Cataloguing-in-Publication data is available from the National Library of Australia

DEDICATION

This work is dedicated to Dr PSB
sibling, inspiration and friend

CONTENTS

Eight Cardinal York & Fr Spotels stories in a timeline.

SAMMY TO THE RESCUE

Charles Cardinal York flexed his shoulders irritably to make the long, scarlet cloak fall down in folds, as it should.

He strove to hold his frustration in check; it wasn't wise to let it run amok today …not with all this in front of him. But, all the same … what's wrong with the idiot?

The MC's supposed to be doing all this! I'll give him a blast – the lazy, young, bloke – this Father …? *Father* …? What the hell *was* his name, anyway? He did tell me.

It was …um … as the old man closed his eyes, searching his mind trying to remember who his new MC was, his clothes were suddenly quickly arranged – with exceptionable speed and efficiency.

He found himself properly dressed – in record time – standing beside the vesting table, just waiting for his scarlet biretta; ready for the procession to begin. He was actually gasping with surprise. The operation had been silent, slick and tension free!

Startled by the unexpected competence of the new secretary-cum-MC, Charles wisely deciding to postpone his complaints, meekly accepting his biretta. As he bowed to the crucifix, then put the biretta on his head, he sneaked a quick side-ways look at this remarkable youngster.

He's a tough-looking character this one! Was he *really* a priest? He looks like a young, unsuccessful, drop-out from the local boxing academy; or, a *thug* – he's got a broken nose. *Yes …* that's more like it; possibly a thug. How interesting!

Could be after the gold and silver chalices. Have to keep an eye on him!

Well, whatever he was, it didn't matter; this one wasn't a sloppy, anaemic, willowy, weepy type, thank God – he'd had enough of those!

"What?" he snapped; suddenly realizing the MC was addressing him.

"Eminence, the photographer has just asked if he may take a shot of you before you begin the procession – just as you are now. What do you think?" Father Samuel Spotels asked quietly.

Charles was surprised at the cultured voice coming from that bruised face.

"Umph!" The cardinal nodded, his lips a thin line. He hated the press even more than he hated …but, he warned himself, *don't* start worrying about *that* … it's too dangerous. Instead, he stood up straight, holding his biretta across the front of his surplice, automatically adopting his usual pose – as he had done for the last twenty-four years.

There were a couple of flashes, and the cardinal heard the photographer say, sotto voce, to the MC: "I'll get a shot later on, when the old goat's actually doing something; mightn't look so poisonous then."

The cardinal smiled grimly. They thought because he was old, he was deaf as well; as a matter of fact, his hearing was perfect. Would to God that everything else was … … but … No, *stop* it! *Don't* go there…

The secretary touched his arm briefly, the procession started. The cardinal watched the procession lead outside: the row of acolytes in their white snowy garments billowing in the gentle air from the open door; the Deacon – he noted, irritably, it was the nervous, fluttery one – a wretched fellow – he'll get everything wrong, as usual; the assisting ministers, his new MC, and then he took his place, alone, at the end of the line.

They came out of the shadows of the huge cathedral into the bright sunshine and the cardinal squinted in the bright light. There were people out here as well, so he automatically raised his right arm in a series of little blessings.

They stopped at the front door of the Church. What on earth was he supposed to do *now*, he asked himself querulously? Oh, yes, that's right … the Asperges!

Thank heavens he didn't have to remember all this now; he couldn't do it. He stood perfectly still: this was the MC's job; he had no intention of helping him. He'd see this morning just how good Father …? Father (whatever his name) is!

Oh, good! He's got it organized. We're off! That's a start anyhow.

The procession passed into the church, and the cardinal noted that it was full to capacity. His heart soared with delight. How wonderful; how good, people are! So many people! *No, no … it wasn't wonderful!* – It just meant there would be more people to see the disgrace if something went wrong! And, it could *so easily*.

He sharply ordered his mind to think of something else.

He made the decision to listen to the singing from the massed choir in the gallery. Hold on! There's something wrong with it? What were they singing?... Good God!

They're churning out the 'Ecce Sacerdos Magnus' Behold the Great Priest – that's the second time they've sung it this morning. Why can't they be imaginative and think up something different for a change? He was so tired of hearing that every time he officiated at something important.

His mind flew off at a tangent. He wondered if *she*, the poor good woman, ever wanted to throw something every time she had to stand, rock still, while they played that dreadful dirge every time *she* did anything – she most probably heard it in her sleep and had night-mares; the poor woman.

The MC was nattering about something again; what was it? Oh, they've reached the sanctuary; well, I can *see that*; silly fellow – I'm not blind. Right … up the three little steps, kneel at the kneeler, stay a few minutes …Oh, *dear! Dear God, help me!* This is *not* a good idea. Quick, think of something else! The *Choir!* That'll do.

He concentrated on the very strange sound coming from the choir gallery which he had noted earlier; what *was* it? The cardinal suddenly recognized the sound as coming from a counter tenor.

He rather liked the unearthly sound of the counter-tenor voice, but today, it certainly *was* unearthly; it was terrible – he was shockingly off-key. It sounded as if the poor chap was being garrotted. The cardinal deliberately closed his mind from the strangling, gurgling sounds from the choir, and seriously pondered his own personal problem.

Yes, he decided, it had to be faced squarely as it definitely *was* a theological problem. It was concerned with the question of a lack of trust … of faith; therefore it *was* his theology – that was now questionable.

Where had he gone wrong? He hadn't been like this in the beginning, had it? *No, he hadn't!* With the ease of the elderly, his mind flew back more than forty years to the day he lay stretched out on the floor, with the other ordinands, being made a priest of the order of Melchisedech forever.

He had firmly believed *then*, there was no obstacle that he could not overcome with his boundless faith; no spiritual mountain, he couldn't climb, but ... ...*now*? Now, it was all a disaster; he would stumble at a slight incline on the path.

But, what could he actually *do*? The press hated him; he knew what they'd write about him if he just walked out. He could see the headlines of the popular papers: '*Roman Catholic Cardinal stalked out of cathedral in a towering rage; it was said he was frothing at the mouth*.' While the sophisticated papers, that pretended to be more intellectual, would write: '*While the actions, and comments of the Cardinal of this city, have given us reasons to be concerned for some years now, it was to be regretted that he left his Cathedral, in such a vulgar manner; leaving nearly one thousand people stranded, half way through a service...*'

No, he couldn't do that. He'd... ...

"What? Oh! Of course, I was just about to stand up." That was not true. He hadn't! He had completely forgotten for a moment *where* he even *was*. He took hold of the kneeler, and pushed himself up ram-rod straight, turned and followed the procession back to the place where he had been at the beginning.

He would then be dressed for the High Mass itself – which, he grumbled – together with the sermon – would take at least another two hours! He *knew*, with a terrible, fearful certainty ... *today*, he would never make it!

As he was given the vestments to put on, the cardinal used the old-fashioned prayers for donning each and every, garment. He loved the old Latin, and still used the Latin formula for the prayers – the Deacon holding the book in front of him, just in case he forgot any of the words.

Not that he ever did; he used these prayers every single day; the book was simply a kind of security blanket – he liked to know it was there.

As they were preparing to dress him, for some reason he thought of his mother, now dead for decades. How thrilled she had been on the day of his ordination as a priest, then the more subdued pleasure when he had become a bishop.

He had been disappointed at her reaction, but thought she would be thrilled when he received word from Rome that he was to be made a cardinal. However he was surprised, again, to hear her say when he phoned her:

"Oh, *Charlie*! You thoughtless boy! How *could* you? You were always so headstrong. This will mean *more* praying for you than I have to do already! I'm an old woman, now; I don't have the time for more. However," he heard her sigh.

"Never mind, what's done is done. I'll do my best."

It must have been her prayers that had kept him going for so long; but what has happened now? Had she, too, abandoned him?

With his mind elsewhere, he took up the amice, saying the prayers automatically, then tying the ends of the tapes together across his chest, he held his arms out to receive the alb, which slipped neatly over his head, his hands going straight into the sleeves. As he muttered the prayers for the maniple. "Merear me Domine......fletus et doloris …" the words suddenly leapt out at him. Well, *that's one thing* that's correct anyhow: fletus et doloris: 'weeping and sorrow' – that's all that's left now – *weeping and sorrow.*

The cardinal winced suddenly; the situation was intensifying: something had to give. He was reaching for the heavy gold Chasuble, when the new secretary suddenly whipped the book from the Deacon's hand and wrote swiftly in it. He then held it before the cardinal, pushing in front of the Deacon, who looked furious – as well as bewildered.

The cardinal, from habit, kept reading softly: "Domine qui dixists… …**DO YOU WANT TO RELIEVE YOUR BLADDER?** …" What on *earth*? Had he misread it? He raised his head and stared into the gentle, understanding eyes of his new secretary.

He nodded, humbly, and whispered: "Yes." The secretary nodded, whispering back: "Leave it to me."

The young man turned to face the rest of the servers and ministers, and clapped his hands quietly. Everyone looked at him.

"The cardinal has just remembered a little theological reference he wishes to check in the wonderful sermon he has written. We will need to check it immediately; it will only take five minutes. Someone inform the choir." He took the cardinal's arm and said quietly: "Come with me, Eminence." They went quickly out the door; the secretary making sure he closed it securely behind them.

"Now, off you go, Eminence," the young man smiled. The cardinal lingered.

"But, how did you know, Father?" he gasped.

The young man laughed. "Bless your innocence, Eminence! It's a common problem for men; my old dad has it."

The cardinal still hesitated: "But, Father, you have been so kind, and I don't even remember your name. Please tell me …I'm very sorry …"

"Not to worry, Eminence. It's Samuel Spotels; easy to remember, rhymes with bottles; just think of the SS. My friends all call me Sammy." He looked at his watch. "Eminence, I don't want to rush you, but you'd better get your skates on. So, off you go, and …er … solve your *Theological* problem."

The cardinal laughed happily. This one, thug or not, was going to be all right; we're going to get on fine; he has a sense of humour!

＊＊＊

In the silence of the Gents, the cardinal made his thanksgiving.

REX VERSUS YORK

It was 1.30 in the morning. The secretary to His Eminence, Charles Cardinal York, Father Sammy Spotels, was sound asleep when the bedside phone shattered the silence with its strident sound.

He woke with a start, grabbed for the phone, dropped the receiver, said a mild swear word, and finally managed to answer.

"Hmmmm … ummpt … hel … hello? Oh … *SO* …you're now the *police*, are you? Now listen carefully Father Black, aka Pongo. I've had enough of you and your false calls. Can't you get it into your thick skull, Pongo, they're *not* funny.

"Last week was bad enough: phoning the fire brigade, telling them the Cathedral was on fire and getting us all out of bed in the early hours of the morning … …

"No! *You* listen to me, you immature, retarded, muscle-head – how you ever became a secretary to a bishop is beyond me – I didn't know you could even *read* let alone write …

"What! You still insist it *is* the police, is it? Good try, Pongo, but, let me tell you, if you ever try this 'impersonating others trick' again, at the next Clergy Conference, I'll take you outside, and you'll have to explain the two black eyes and a broken nose to your boss! I might even tell your bishop about these calls.

"You might remember I was the boxing champ at university – you lump head … you …

"*WHAT* did you say? What do you *mean*? Assault and Battery, Blackmail with menaces? *What are you talking about?* … You mean to say you really *ARE* the police? Good grief! … Well, how was I supposed to know when I've got an idiot priest ringing me up at all hours of the night, thinking it's funny? … I suppose so; yes … well I'm sorry, Officer, I didn't mean to imply that *the police* were immature, retarded or muscle-heads. … …Well, what do you want? … Of *course*, I'm the cardinal's secretary … My name? Father Sammy Spotels … Well, I didn't choose it; my mother chose the 'Sammy' bit... Yes, *believe* me, I *do* know – to my cost – the old joke – the 'SS' Hitler, et al.

"As a matter of fact, Officer, my mother named me *after* the SS … No, it's true; she did! She thought it meant 'Silly Sausage'; she said that's what I looked like when I was born.

"But, I've had to tell you *my* name, what, may I ask, is *yours*? … Oh, Inspector *David*! Do I call you David? … Oh, it's a last name? What is your first name? … *REX*? It *isn't*? … It *is*! … Well, who are you to talk about my mother's choice of names? Your mother must have had delusions of grandeur, hadn't she?

"You don't know what I'm talking about? Never mind, let's forget that, we can't help our names … …

"Excuse me interrupting, Inspector, but what is that loud shouting in the background, it sounds familiar? Would you hold the mobile out so I can hear it better? Thank you … Good God! … *It's* the *Cardinal*! Where in the name of heaven *are you*?

"*WHERE?* … Behind the big supermarket and he's … *WHERE?* … In the *dumpster* behind the store, up to his waist in garbage?

"My head is reeling – this is worse than Pongo! *No, of course, the cardinal shouldn't be there!* What's he doing in a *dumpster* for the love of God? … Would you repeat that please, Inspector?

You're not having me on? … He's standing over a *dead policeman* who's been murdered, you think? Dear God, can this all be true? …Yes, of course I'll be there as quickly as I can; I'll take my motorbike...

"Inspector, I sincerely beg of you: be gentle with the old man; he wouldn't hurt a fly and he's as innocent as a lamb … Well, that's the truth … despite the fact that I don't know what the hell he's doing at this hour of the night, in such a dreadful place, and – in a dumpster! I'll be as quick as I can."

Father Sammy Spotels jumped out of bed, pulled on his shoes and then grabbed his cassock – that would hide his pyjamas – his black leather jacket, his helmet and was ready in a few minutes.

He ran to the garage under the Bishop's House, leapt on his motorbike, and roared away into the darkness.

When he arrived at the big supermarket store, he thought the dumpster would most likely be in the alley behind the store, so he rode there.

Sammy found a number of police standing about, but his eyes became riveted on the biggest dumpster. There was a police spotlight shining on the cardinal who was standing up in the middle of the garbage, with a coil of what looked like wilted celery hanging from that wretched Roman hat which he persisted in wearing.

He called it his 'Father Brown Hat,' after he had seen the old black and white film starring Alec Guinness, as Father Brown. Sammy Spotels thought it looked like a flat pancake, or a model of a flying saucer. Sammy noticed the cardinal was wearing his red cassock with a black cloak which came to his ankles.

As soon as the prelate saw his secretary, he shouted at him:

"Sammy did you bring the oils?"

Before the secretary could answer, Inspector Rex David thrust himself forward. He was a bulky man with a dark heavy face, thick eyebrows, a rather full nose, and sensual lips. His eyes were black; he was not happy.

"This is no time for oils; we're not cooking anything …"

"Take no notice of him, Sammy," shouted the Cardinal, "go straight back and get the oils quickly; the young policeman's still alive but won't be much longer." Sammy immediately revved up his bike, and as the inspector shouted: 'Oh, no you *don't*', he DID! Sammy was soon a fading trail of exhaust smoke, as he tore back to the cathedral for the Holy Oils.

Back at the dumpster, the cardinal was assuring the inspector that his secretary was not fleeing the country; would be back in a few minutes. As that was the case, he demanded that he be left alone, as he had lots of prayers to say for this poor dying young policeman, lying on a bed of rotting cabbages, and overturned yoghurt.

Within a few minutes the secretary had returned, and Cardinal York anointed the young policeman with gentle, sure fingers, while Father Spotels held the hand of the dying man gently, answering the responses.

The police were embarrassed and some lifted their caps in respect for their colleague. It was only a couple of minutes later that the cardinal lifted his head and told the men: "I'm sorry, he's gone. May flights of angels lead him to Paradise."

He folded the young dead hands together and took out his identity card from the policeman's pocket. He looked at the photo of a beautiful young woman which had been in the pocket as well. Her name was written underneath the photo, with the words: 'my beautiful wife'. The cardinal read the name and his eyebrows rose.

He turned to Inspector David. "Excuse me, Inspector, what did you say your name was?"

"You know it, you old fool. It's Inspector David."

"I don't think your mother, God rest her soul, actually named you '*Inspector*'. I mean your first name."

"What do you want with my first name?" The Inspector had had enough of this ridiculous charade. The secretary broke in:

"Eminence, I know it. It's *Rex*."

The Cardinal rose to his full height and glared at the policemen.

"Aha! Now listen to me. Detective Constable Uri Costello has been shot twice with a police revolver; the two shots were fired from below, as he was standing here in the dumpster – the exit wounds indicate that. Constable Uri Costello was ordered to be here, on his own, to spy on the drug gang which uses this alleyway for their collection and distribution sessions.

"He was sent here alone on a dangerous and impossible mission, by an officer who was trying to seduce the young man's good wife. She had declared to the officer, that she would never be unfaithful to her husband; she would be faithful even to death.

"The only way to fulfil the officer's evil desires, was to kill the husband. It *is* a case of *Murder*. After the young constable had taken up his position, the officer came here before the gang arrived, shot the young man, and then returned to headquarters."

The cardinal lifted his arm and pointed dramatically at Inspector David.

"Arrest Inspector Rex David immediately, for the murder of Detective Constable Uriah Costello." Then, in a more homely tone: "What are you waiting for Sammy, tackle the brute!"

The police moved in on their superior officer. Inspector David started to sweat heavily. He looked up at the strange figure in the garbage dumpster, looking for all the world like one of the prophets in the books that his old Jewish mother had shown him as a child. He attempted to lie:

"I didn't mean to actually kill him …"

"Liar," shouted the old cardinal. "You carefully planned every movement. If I had not been taking a little walk around the city because I couldn't sleep, you would have got away with it. But," again, he pointed at Rex David. "If you had only lived as your good parents hoped, you would have fled a mile from any attempt on the life of a man called Uriah."

"How did you know all this? And why on earth should I have avoided that name?" The Inspector's collapse was complete.

He was so shocked at the unexpected revelation of his crime, that he let the officers take his gun away and put handcuffs on his wrists without resistance.

"Oh, read your Scriptures, you silly man." The cardinal turned away. "Get the ambulance; this poor boy can be taken away now." He then climbed down out of the dumpster.

"Take me home, please Sammy. We've got that awful visit to the Children's Home in the morning early."

***

The cardinal and his secretary went to the motorbike which the cardinal hated. However he held his tongue this time.

As soon as they had begun to move – this time very sedately – the cardinal leaned forward and whispered to his secretary. "Sammy, I need to go to Confession."

"Can't it wait?"

"No, it cannot. Keep driving, but carefully please. Bless me father – *no don't bother taking your hand from the handlebars* – I have sinned. I have pretended that it was I who was able to deduce the facts about the murder …"

"Good grief, wasn't it?"

"Not entirely, Father. You see the leader of the drug gang was once my altar-boy – God have mercy on him, breaks his mother's heart – and he saw me out walking and called me over and told me all about it; he also told me that the young man was still alive.

"You see the gangster knew I'd want to absolve the dying man from his sins – so the poor gangster can't be all bad, can he? He said there wasn't much time left, he thought. The gang had seen it all, although the police inspector didn't *see them*.

"They wouldn't, and *couldn't*, give evidence, so I had to do something for poor Uri Costello – I've known him since he first learnt to play marbles. But, Father, I've been guilty of pride and vanity for I did enjoy myself up there in the dumpster, and that was wrong and sinful of me. I humbly beg pardon and absolution from you, my ghostly father."

The secretary was trying desperately hard not to laugh. So, the old villain had fooled everyone including him. But, he was also touched by the simplicity and goodness of the old man and, turning slightly, he raised his right arm to give the absolution – totally forgetting he was on a bike: "Ego te Absolvo a peccatis tuis …" That was as far as he got. The bike spun madly out of control and the machine and passengers parted company in a dramatic, and quite spectacular manner.

***

Sammy woke up in a hospital bed. He was aware that something was wrong with one arm; he couldn't move it easily. He gingerly tried to move his legs but they seemed to be all right. He opened his eyes to see the worried, anxious face of the old cardinal leaning over him. There were tears in the old man's eyes.

He had escaped without a scratch.

"Oh, Sammy," he whispered, "I've been so worried that you weren't going to make it."

"Aha! Just as I thought! You'd actually miss me, wouldn't you?"

"To be honest, Father … … no. But *today*, yes, indeed. You see, Father, you didn't give me a penance after my confession last night, so I need you to give me one now."

Sammy was irritated by the answer, so easing his aching arm, he spoke severely. "Your sins are indeed wicked and should be of great concern to you. Your penance is to make a genuine promise to God – binding under grave sin – that you will *not* take solitary walks at night in the city for the next three months. Is that clear?"

"Perfectly clear. Anything else?"

"Yes, you looked at the photo of the young policeman's wife. You told me her name was written on it. What was it?"

"Really, I thought you, with all your fancy degrees, Father, would have worked that out for yourself. If you didn't spend so much time fooling around with that wretched motorbike-contraption of yours and attend to your studies … Oh you young chaps! That was dead easy … it was *Bathsheba*."

The cardinal moved to the door. "Enough of all that! I'll wait in the hallway, Father, while you get dressed."

"Get dressed?"

"Of course, there's no need for you to be lying about in a hospital bed all day; you've only got a sprained wrist and a bit of concussion. You must have forgotten we have a busy schedule today. We have that awful visit to the dreaded kids' Home; you can't expect me to face those monsters on my own!

"You can show them your arm in its bandages, and make up wonderful stories about how you hurt it rescuing a trapped king who was being eaten by tigers, or something; I'll be inside inspecting the books – pretending that I understand them ... Now, hurry up; I'll drive that bike-thing – it wasn't damaged."

Alone in the hospital room Sammy climbed out of the bed awkwardly with his painful left wrist, and suddenly began to laugh! Who would have thought that working for this extraordinary old man could be so exciting? *And* so funny! There was something new and unexpected happening every single day!

He suddenly stood stock-still. *WHAT* did he say? He'd drive? No, No, No, *NO!* Never again! Not on your life! He nearly killed us last time!

"Eminence," he called through the closed door. "I'll be there in a minute. Don't worry, I'll drive; I'm fine, really fine. Be with you in a moment."

Outside the door, standing in the corridor, Charles smiled. He thought that would do the trick!

THE CLASS REUNION

Detective Inspector Naseby, accompanied by Detective Constable Costello, found it more difficult than they had expected when they turned up at the cathedral offices, demanding to see the Cardinal Archbishop of the city, Charles Cardinal York.

Firstly, there was the obstacle of the outer office, presided over by the enchantingly pretty, but utterly ruthless, Miss Amy Wright, with her assistant, Janet Nubbs. The inspector was subjected to such an intense interrogation by Miss Wright that left him wondering if they could adopt her technique down at the station. It was only when they had produced enough identification to satisfy Miss Wright that they were permitted to go to stage two in the process – that is, to the Cardinal's secretary's office.

Miss Wright tapped lightly on the office door, opened it and announced:

"Father Spotels, a Detective Inspector Naseby and a Detective Constable Costello to see you."

Father Sammy Spotels stood up to greet his visitors politely, when he was suddenly aware of both the name and the appearance of the young constable. He was confused – his mind was obviously playing tricks on him.

He hastily tried to pull himself together, and turning to the inspector, the first thing he noticed was the large nose on the policeman's face. He tried frantically to remember what name Miss Wright had said – it had started with N … He hazarded a guess: "Come in Inspector Noseby," and politely motioned the men to the chairs.

"Not Noseby, Naseby!" angrily replied the Detective. Then turning to his constable, he spoke sharply: "Take notes, Costello – might need them in court."

Now Father Sammy Spotels, admirable priest in every way that he was, was not going to be put down by any rude policeman. He immediately pressed down a little key on his intercom, which connected him with Miss Wright's office: "Miss Wright, please come in immediately; you are to take notes; we might need them in court when we sue."

There was dead silence at this impasse; the men waited for Miss Wright who, poised and unflappable as usual, came in and took her place in the corner, with her pad on her knee.

The inspector realised that he had not been very wise in the approach he had taken with this tough character, and tried to regain the upper ground. "She said you were very busy, yet all you're doing is reading the newspapers – wasted a whole thirty minutes I have."

Father Spotels glared at the man. "Not busy! I'd just like you to have to do this for just one morning."

"Do what?"

"Go through all this junk, making notes of every single thing I think the cardinal should know; what every silly jumped-up politician said, or *didn't* say; what the fashionable so-called celebrities – who are totally moronic and, consequently, cannot *speak* English, let alone *write* it – said on every subject, from the morality of genetic research to global warming."

"But, you've got the *Entertainment* section open before you," protested the inspector. Father Sammy Spotels kept trying to concentrate on the inspector, but his eyes kept darting to the constable. However, he managed to continue the conversation.

"Indeed, I have. It's easy to see why you're called a detective!" Sammy then dropped his sarcastic tone, and was suddenly serious.

"Look here, Inspector, the cardinal's a very important man – you must know that. As such, he's invited to all kinds of ritzy functions, with important people from all walks of life. Now, part of my job is to keep files on just about all the so-called 'important' people that the cardinal is likely to meet; I keep them while they are alive, and then the files go to Miss Wright.

"For the live people, I have to be able to tell the cardinal, before he goes to a meeting, whether the host is a keen golfer, or loves sailing; whether he likes Opera or, whether he's into Bridge, Chess, Racing cars, whatever … you know … just to help him to have *something* to say to these people."

"Good heavens! Is that what the VIPs talk about at important meetings?"

"Of course," the secretary replied, surprised, "you didn't think they ever said anything really *important*, did you? Why, only the other day, when the poor cardinal had to attend a special meeting called to discuss the outbreak of war in a certain place, he complained to me afterwards, that all the chief 'Big-Wig' wanted to talk about were his varicose veins!"

"But what do you keep the *dead* files for?"

"For the Remembrance Services that the cardinal has to attend; or, if he has to entertain a visiting foreign prelate of some country, or other, he can pay a tribute to the previous president, or dictator, or monarch, or … Get the drift?"

"Well, I never! Is that a fact?" the inspector shook himself, his big nose going from right to left. "However, that's got nothing to do with why we're here. "

"Before you begin, Inspector," Sammy interrupted. "I'm sorry, but I have to ask your constable a question – I can't put it off any longer; it's distracting me." Sammy looked closely at the young man who appeared to be about thirty. "Constable haven't we met somewhere before? I didn't quite catch your name. It isn't Costello is it?"

The constable smiled hugely. "It certainly is, and to my knowledge, we have never met before."

"But I held your hand when the cardinal was anointing you, as you were *dying*!" Sammy shouted; then added savagely, "and let me tell you something, Buster. I'm not in the habit of holding men's hands, so when it happened, I most certainly *do* remember it. So, spill the beans son: how *can* you be here, when you're *dead*." In her corner, Miss Wright uttered a little scream. The constable turned to her.

"It's all right, Miss Wright, I'm not dead. That was my brother Uriah, my name is Bello Luigi."

"*Bello* Luigi Costello?" queried Father Spotels, "that's as weird as your brother's name."

"My mother's fault, Father," laughed Bello. "She reads these books, you see ..."

The young constable was rudely interrupted by his superior officer. "Can it, will you? Could we get on with the investigation?" The constable apologized, and the inspector continued.

"Look sir, we received a complaint about the cardinal, and we have to follow it up. It most probably is nothing but ..."

"What is it?"

The Inspector felt foolish, so he spoke harshly: "It is claimed that you were riding your motorbike in a dangerous manner – with the cardinal on the back – around about eight o'clock last night, and with that long 'walking-stick-thing' he carries, you actually smashed one of the lights in Riordan Street down near the Opera House. And, if that's not enough, several cars reported that they received large scratches on the sides of their cars." The inspector nodded his head at the priest and winked slyly.

"Look, sir, just tell me it's a load of nonsense, and we'll be on our way; there was no real harm done – the motorists will get their money from their insurance, and as for the light globe – a few dollars would cover that."

"But I can't do that, Inspector," Sammy said regretfully. "You see, it's correct. I didn't know the cardinal was carrying his crosier when he got on the back of my bike last night, fully dressed – mitre and all – as we dashed off to the Opera House where the cardinal performed on stage, in Act I Scene Two of the Opera 'Attila'… It's by Verdi, you know, Inspector …"

"Sir," gasped the policeman, "I'm not feeling well. I'm obviously missing something; I don't know what the hell – excuse me Miss – you're talking about. What *stage* performance? What was the cardinal doing on the stage of the *Opera* House? Why was he fully dressed – with his pointy hat and all – on the back of a *motor* bike?

"No, this is all beyond me … would it be possible to get a glass of water?"

Miss Wright hastened to do as asked. Father Sammy Spotels took pity on the detective inspector. He spoke kindly to the policeman.

"Look here, Inspector, it's a pretty weird story, I know. But, it all makes sense in the end. I mean, we didn't know we'd be going to the Opera House at all …It all happened so suddenly. I'll tell you, blow by blow, what happened … This is how it all came about:

"My story actually begins the day before yesterday – that is Wednesday morning."

***

Father Spotel's narrative:

I had finished the work on the newspapers and been buzzed to let me know the cardinal was ready for our usual morning office routine. I gathered up my notes, and went into his office. We exchanged greetings and set to work.

The cardinal has a tremendous memory, and rarely uses notes, but he keeps a pad near him as I speak, so that if something he thinks important is said, he can jot it down in the strange shorthand he uses.

As I went through the political news, I really paid no heed to his usual derogatory remarks about the people involved – they were, as per usual, that is, 'Why doesn't that pestilential politician become a beachcomber – that's all he's fit for?'; 'Isn't that old idiot dead yet?' and other felicitous remarks. It was when I got on to the Entertainment section that is of relevance to you, Inspector, so I'll skip to that … I said to the Cardinal:

"Eminence, didn't you tell me that you knew Terry Devlin; that he had been with you in the seminary, training for the priesthood, at one time?" The cardinal's face grew sorrowful.

"Poor Terry! Broke his mother's heart, it did. Only stayed one year in the seminary, then left. I knew he wasn't for the priesthood; he should have left, but, afterwards …"

"Yes?"

"Oh, terrible things, Sammy, terrible! Did some tumbling and tap dancing act in some music hall, or other …vaudeville, I think."

"Vaudeville, Eminence, was before your time …" The cardinal interrupted me, saying darkly:

"At my age, Sammy, there is practically *nothing* before my time, except perhaps Adam and Eve."

"That's as may be, but Terry Devlin certainly didn't do vaudeville acts. What *did* he do?"

"Oh, didn't he? Well, possibly, it was something about sword swallowing or juggling, or something," the cardinal exclaimed impatiently: "I don't really *know*. I only know that he ended up very badly; but he was once a great friend and I pray for him daily."

"Well he didn't end up too badly, Eminence," I was happy to announce. "He is *Sir Terence Devlin* now, and he's a pretty famous Opera singer – past his prime now, of course."

The cardinal's eyes were goggling. "Sir Terence? Oh, isn't that a kindness of God. I must ring his mother." He then gasped with annoyance. "Sammy, I've done it again! I'd forgotten the good woman's been dead for at least thirty years – a bad sign ... Never mind ... Sir Terry, eh? Doesn't that beat the band! And he's appearing in some musical, or other, is he? What part is he playing?"

I had been waiting for this question. "Oh, nothing much, Eminence, only that of Pope St. Leo the Great!"

"*WHAT*? Is it a religious play?"

"Well, in a way you could say it is. You see, it's a famous Opera by an Italian chap called Verdi, and Attila the Hun calls off sacking Rome because of the intervention of that saintly, and wonderful Bishop, Leo. And, your old friend is playing the non-singing role of that *saint*." The cardinal was scandalized.

"The nerve of him – after the sort of life he's led! ... But why is that of particular interest to me here, in this city this morning?"

"Because, Eminence, he's actually performing down at the Opera House, five minutes away from us. Tonight is the opening night of the Opera, 'Attila.'"

"Well, well, I never! Very interesting." The Cardinal sat up straight then picked up his notes. "Right! That's enough gossiping; we've got a lot of things to do today Sammy, and then tonight ... remind me again ..." I looked at my diary:

"The six o'clock Mass for the Men's Society. Remember, Eminence, there'll only be a small number present – about one hundred, or so – before their annual meeting. You are not attending the meeting; we'll be finished by eight o'clock, so it won't be too tiring for you. Your sermon is typed up – jolly good if I may say so – and Miss Wright will have it for you when we come back from the meeting of the School Funding Board."

"Thank you Sammy, now regarding the Funding details of the school meeting …"

The meeting continued, Inspector, as on any other ordinary morning. It was at night that everything went haywire.

***

At seven-forty five that evening, the cardinal followed the servers, and me – who acts as his secretary, and his MC as well – back into the sacristy to unvest after Mass. As we entered the large room, the cardinal's cell phone started its infernal ringing.

Cardinal York has this thing about *bells*, so had chosen to have, as his call-sign, a peal of clashing bells clanging away each time his phone rang. The problem with this was that he usually forgot to turn it off most times when we went onto the sanctuary, in the cathedral. Thus, in the middle of High Mass, there could erupt a gigantic peal of bells emanating from the cardinal's trouser pocket. As he wore a microphone clipped to his vestments, the mike picked up the sound, and it reverberated throughout the entire huge cathedral.

I've often thought people in the cathedral must think that the hunch-back of Notre Dame was real, not fiction, and that we've got him locked up in the bell-tower, where he swings, madly and insanely, on the great bells, whenever the mood takes him.

The cardinal picked up his phone and said grumpily: "Yes?

… Cheryl Stoking? … The what? … The diver? No, I'm not interested in aquatic performers …" I grabbed the phone out of the cardinal's hand.

"Miss Stoking, this is Father Spotels, the cardinal's secretary. Yes, I'm sorry, a very bad line … Naturally, I know who *you* are, Miss Stoking – surely there isn't a person in the entire world who doesn't know the famous and wonderful Opera diva, Cheryl Stoking … Well, of course we will, anything we can do to help … Oh, I *am* sorry, he is my cardinal's old friend; very ill, you said? What exactly was Sir Terence's message? … … *Really*? Would you please hold for one moment, while I relay that to the cardinal? … Thank you …" I turned to the cardinal.

"Eminence, it seems that your old friend and fellow student, Terry Devlin, is dying, and is asking for you personally. He said to give you a special message. He said: 'tell Charlie, I'm a goner, and I'm cashing in my chips, but there's sticky problems to clean up, such as six marriages and … um … other things. Tell him he must come to save me, to pay me back, for I know he cheated at the first Logic exam we did in first year – because he copied from my paper, and we both got it wrong.'"

The cardinal started to blush, and blustered to cover up:

"Is all this serious, Father? Is he actually dying? Ask that Choking woman how long does he have?" I picked up the phone again.

"Miss Stoking? Sorry to keep you. I have told the cardinal everything and he asked how long do you think Sir Terence has? … Oh my God! Truly? Just fifteen minutes. Right! We'll do our best anyway. Tell him we're coming …What's that? He asked that the cardinal come *fully vested*? That's pretty peculiar … very well."

"Yes, I heard, Sammy. Fully dressed, huh? That's just like the silly chap; he'd make a drama even out of his own death! Oh, well, we'll have to take the bike; we'd never get through the traffic at this time of night. Fifteen minutes! Dear God have mercy on us, and on the dying poor man – dreadful humbug that he actually is, really! Right, grab the holy oils, and off we go."

Well, we actually ran to the garage beneath the cathedral – the cardinal's pretty nippy on his pins – and I had completely forgotten that the cardinal was still carrying his crosier. We had no time to go back, and as it is solid silver, we couldn't just dump it – we were stuck with it. For the first time I was glad that the cardinal had chosen, against my wishes, to wear a particularly high mitre on his head with precious stones glittering in it.

I objected to it, as it was too tight for his head, and I always had a terrible job, taking it off and putting it on, during Solemn High Mass, but he persisted in using it, and now I was glad. With it so tight, there was no danger of it coming off while we tore through the streets at a fearful rate.

The cardinal put the wretched crosier horizontally across his knees, and held it and my belt with one hand, and the flaps of his mitre with the other. As we tore through the crowded streets, there were several loud metallic noises, and a lot of swearing from other cars, but, to tell the truth, I was driving so fast I was not really paying attention to the other vehicles on the road.

We arrived at the Opera House, and went charging in the back entrance, explaining our presence as we ran to the Green Room, where apparently Sir Terence had been taken. The stage manager met us, and shouted some meaningless greeting which meant nothing to us. Something about: 'Thank God, you've brought your own costume!' while the famous diva Cheryl Stoking stood, looking magnificent, in her wonderful costume examining her face in a mirror.

Her face was painted with an extraordinary amount of 'blueness' around the eyes. The cardinal muttered to me as we raced along: "Why does that Choking woman have blue around her eyes? A birthmark perhaps?" He never received an answer, as we had arrived at the Green Room by then, and Cardinal York had rushed in to his old friend whom he found lying on a fancy velvet lounge looking dramatically ill. The cardinal took the holy oils from me and told me, and a group of stage people, brusquely, to 'get the hell out,' so we did.

We huddled in the hall. Five minutes later the cardinal came out looking very serious.

"Father Spotels, you and I are about to make our stage debut!"

"We're what?" I shouted. "Have you gone completely insane?"

The stage manager bustled up. "They're ready. Just follow the monks and the other priests, and you, son, stay close to the understudy. When you get to Attila the Hun, he will fall at the bishop's feet; the bishop will bless him, and then he will follow the procession off the other side of the stage. All understood?"

"No!" I shouted, just as the cardinal said: "Perfectly."

The costume manager rushed up to us as we joined this weird procession. He grabbed me: "No you can't go on like that; it's too ordinary; put this cape over your black skirt – that'll look more authentic." Before I could get out of it, I was walking on to the Opera stage beside the cardinal, who was looking magnificent in his very tall mitre and robes, with me, at his side, looking as if I were a prize fighter dressed up in his mother's old tatty sequinned evening cape.

The cardinal kept whispering to me as we walked slowly across that endless stage: "They do this better than we do, Sammy; where do all these monks come from? I thought there was a shortage of vocations? Does their Abbot know what they're doing, I wonder? Goodness, isn't the singing magnificent, and so loud! I had no idea there'd be so much *noise*!"

The 'noise' was thrillingly magnificent: the whole chorus were singing their heads off, the orchestra going flat out, while the greatest noise seemed to be coming from a chap, with horns on his helmet, in the centre of the stage. He turned to see us, and began uttering cries of what seemed like surprise mingled with anguish.

The cardinal followed the procession to Attila. Charles Cardinal York had a magnificent voice himself, though at his age, naturally enough, it was slightly cracked. He faltered for a moment, as he stared at the opera singer, who was now on his knees at his feet. The cardinal looked startled, and then his great voice boomed out:

"Ar-tur-o!" and, unconsciously mimicking the sounds around him, *he sang the name on three notes.* The orchestra faltered, and stopped.

A deadly silence permeated the 3,000 seat auditorium. Attila was crying; the cardinal was bent over him, and then I noticed his hand rising slowly in benediction. Being a bishop, without thinking, the cardinal began to *sing* the benediction, as he usually did at the Latin High Mass: "Benedictio Dei omnipotentis, Patris + et Filii, et Spiritus Sancti, descend---------." He laid his hand on Attila's head, and gently raised him by the arm up to his feet again.

Both the cardinal and the singer seemed oblivious to the terrifying, total silence enveloping this huge building. I was nearly fainting with sheer terror – stuck in the middle of that god-awful stage – the size of a football stadium.

I think it was sheer funk that made me bellow out: "*A...men.*" I've had to do that many times at Mass, when the choir has failed to respond when they should.

At the end of my long note, the first violin began to replay the last section of what Attila had been singing; the rest of the orchestra joined in; the tenor, brought back to the present by the sound, picked up the line, and then his glorious voice rang out in triumphant joy.

The cardinal and I then followed the procession to stage left, and found ourselves back in the corridor.

I was dripping with sweat, and ripping the tatty cape from my body, I grabbed the arm of my boss. "Eminence, what about Sir Terence? Do we need to go back there? Is he dead?"

To my amazement the cardinal swore.

"*Damn* fellow! I should have known! He always was a tricky bloke; nothing wrong with him – strong as an ox; just sprained his ankle and wanted an understudy to go on, for one night only. If they got another chap to play the Bishop, then the precious Sir Terence would have got the sack! Hasn't changed a bit; was always getting other people to do his work back at the seminary!"

"But," I asked, "what about the other fellow – the 'Arturo Hun' chap on stage?"

The cardinal's eyes glowed with happiness and satisfaction. "What a surprise that was, Sammy! That was Young Arturo, the son of another great old friend of mine who was also at the seminary with me – he left in the second year, I think. I knew he had a very gifted son, but we lost touch. The boy's father's dead now, and his son, Young Arturo, is singing the lead in this Opera – his first big lead in his own town.

"When I saw the young man I received a shock; for a moment I thought I was seeing my dear old friend whom I knew was dead – the son is the living image of his father. That's why I called out his name. But when he saw me he recognized me instantly, and, good lad that he is, knelt down immediately and asked for my blessing – very moving, actually.

"We both really forgot where we were; I invited him to the cathedral tomorrow for afternoon tea, and it was only when you *bellowed* out your frightful 'Amen', that we realised where we were – and that we were not alone."

We had reached the bike by this time. The cardinal perched

himself complacently on the back, still with that blasted crosier in his hand.

"I did *not* bellow," I objected.

"You did, you know full well you *did*."

"Well, if I did, it was to help you get out of the mess you'd got us both in."

"That's as may be; let's get moving …"

"No, I want to know; how did young Arturo recognize you?"

The Cardinal interrupted me. "Good Gracious me! What does this silly chap want?" I turned to see the director of the Opera running to catch us.

"Good work, chaps! That was splendid. We'll keep in that 'ad lib' business you did tonight – the crowd loved it. Anytime you want to earn a bit of pocket money as extras – that goes for both of you …"

I was angry at this affront to the cardinal. "I'll have you know, sir, that this is a *real* bishop, not a *pretend* one!"

The director laughed loudly, and slapped his sides. "Oh, you are *so* good! A *real* one! Off you go; you actors tell the biggest whoppers ever!" And laughing, he went back into the building. The cardinal, totally unperturbed, turned back to me.

"You were asking, Father?"

"How young Arturo recognized you instantly on stage tonight?" The cardinal actually looked slightly embarrassed.

"Well, it seems that his father spoke about me a lot, and they actually had my official portrait-photo in their hall …"

"To frighten the burglars, I suppose …"

"Sammy, Sammy, Sammy," Cardinal York chided sadly, shaking his head. "I have to tell you that I'm very concerned about you. You see, I shouldn't be telling you this, but I have an important report to write on you soon. It could be that it concerns your promotion …"

"You don't mean that anyone would be mad enough to think of promoting me, do you? Good God!" I shouted in amazement.

"Believe me, Father, I share your astonishment! ... However," continued the cardinal, "I'm beginning to think that you do not have sufficient 'gravitas.'"

"*Gravitas*?"

"It means ..."

"For heavens' sake, I *know* what it means! Well, I think I have enough 'gravitas' as anyone needs. I don't go tumbling somersaults around the office in my undies, do I?"

"No, Sammy, but that's only because I won't let you."

I gave a theatrical sigh. "That's true, of course," I answered sadly, and we both collapsed in laughter. "OK Eminence, hold on to your mitre; keep that blasted crosier upright – might be safer that way – and it's back to the cathedral for us. And," I added firmly, "when we get there, we're going to have a small sherry before bed – to mark our first, and *last* appearance on the Opera stage!"

With the Cardinal chuckling behind me I drove as fast as I dared back to the Cathedral.

***

Father Spotels stopped, and paused for a few moments. He then declared: "And, that, Inspector Naseby, is the whole story!" He had kept his eyes down on his clasped hands all the time he had been speaking, trying to remember every detail that the inspector had demanded.

He now lifted his head, and was puzzled to see both Miss Wright and Constable Costello shaking with laughter and holding hands, while the inspector's eyes were like saucers.

"You don't mean to tell me that was what actually *happened*?" shouted the highly incensed policeman.

"Of course, that's what I was trying to do: tell you every detail of the whole evening – it's the complete truth."

"I don't believe it!" The Inspector shook his head. "No, I cannot believe it; it's like something from a Marx brothers' film." He stood up and motioned to the constable. "Come on Constable, let's get out of this place. I'm writing this down as a case of 'mistaken identity'. No one would ever believe it, if I told the truth."

He nodded curtly to Father Spotels and Miss Wright, and marched out of the room. The constable lingered.

"Seven o'clock all right, Amy?"

"Fine, Bello, but it'll have to be fish, it's Friday."

"Suits me – always fish on Fridays for me too."

As the two people left the office, the buzzer went and the cardinal's voice came clearly through the intercom:

"Well, if you're finished sleeping in there, Father Spotels, dreaming of a new career in Opera, may I remind you that we have not yet begun the day's work! You most probably have forgotten, but the Armenian Patriarch is calling for a courtesy visit this morning, and staying to lunch …"

"No, I haven't forgotten. I've been busy. The police have been here, and I've just saved you from being arrested."

"What a pity! It would have been exciting, and I wouldn't have had to eat a vegetarian lunch …"

"A vegetarian lunch?"

"Ah! I see you've forgotten haven't you? This Patriarch is a vegetarian, so it's all salads with nuts and things – can't stand the stuff."

"No, it's *you* who has it wrong, Eminence; *this* Patriarch is *not* the vegetarian, he's the one into model aeroplanes …"

"Well, get in here quickly and brief me, Sammy. Security has just advised me that he has entered the crypt with his entourage."

Sammy grabbed his notes and fled to the cardinal's office.

THE GREAT SANTA
BANK HEIST

"Well, I am surprised, Inspector Naseby," Father Sammy Spotels remarked as he ushered his visitor into his office. "Last time you were here you said you hoped never to have to set foot in this place again …"

"And I meant it!" snapped the inspector. "Last time was enough to send one crazy in this lunatic asylum you've got here … but," he paused for breath, "needs must! Another of your ridiculous fellow-priests up to no good …"

"Impossible!" protested Sammy indignantly, although he had a sinking feeling in his stomach – who could it be *this* time, he wondered? "As if a fellow priest would be up to no good …"

"No, it's no use you trying to bamboozle me again with words, as you did on the last occasion. We've got him in the lock-up at the station – him in his fancy Santa suit."

"In his *WHAT*?" exclaimed Sammy, genuinely startled. "And where *was* this fellow in a Santa suit may I ask, before you nabbed him?"

"On the roof near the chimney, of course, where the hell do you think he would have been?"

Sammy paused. This looked like becoming one of their usual

peculiar interactions with the law. He thought it prudent to use a neutral tone. "Let's sit down, Inspector, and please tell me all about it; I honestly don't know what the dickens you're talking about."

"I'll sit down, but don't think you'll befuddle me again, you young … Well, never mind that … we found this bloke dressed all in red with white fur, and he was …"

"Yes, I've got that. This chap was acting as Santa, and he was up on the roof near a chimney. Well, as I remember from my childhood, that's where Santa's supposed to be, isn't it?"

"It depends on the chimney," the inspector said enigmatically, his eye-brows coming together over his large nose.

"The chimney?" Sammy was lost. "Where *was* the chimney?"

"It was the chimney that leads down to the vaults of the bank."

"Oh, that does make a big difference, I can see that, Inspector, but what has that got to do with us? Why must it be a priest? It could be anybody."

The inspector looked triumphant. "Ah hah! I've got you now! We know it's a priest because he gave *your* name, as a reference, to prove it."

"He, *WHAT*?" Sammy actually stood up in his shock. "Who the hell is this bloke …?" but even as he asked the question, a dreadful suspicion was beginning to form in Sammy's mind. He cast his mind around furiously, trying to think of any *sane* reason – for the person he suspected – being on the rooftop of a bank! The inspector continued:

"He said he would only give me his nickname – from Uni, it seems – and it was …"

"No, don't tell me, Inspector. It wasn't that idiot Father Pongo Black again was it?" Sammy sat down again, hardly bearing to hear his suspicions confirmed.

"Well I don't know about the surname, but the 'Pongo' bit is correct. Then," the policeman's eyes glittered in triumph, "he *is* telling the truth; he *is* one of you lot?"

Father Spotels closed his eyes: the trouble that that crazy priest had caused was enough to send you round the bend – and the idiot always had the nerve to think what he did was funny! He'd give him 'funny' next time they met – which actually looked like being sooner than he expected! The inspector stood up and spoke officially:

"Reverend Spotels, I have to inform you that the gentleman, now in our cells at the Station, has declared that you are his confederate, and so ..."

Sammy again leapt to his feet. "He didn't! ... He couldn't! ... He wouldn't ... would he? ... He *didn't*, did he?"

"He *did*! Before witnesses too!"

"I must inform the Cardinal at once; he must be notified of this scandalous situation ..." Sammy's voice was cut short by the cardinal's voice coming through the intercom.

"Where the dickens are you, Sammy, off robbing a bank or something? Come in, I need you; I have to count all this money we've ..."

The inspector actually shouted in his excitement. "Now we've got you! The pair of you! Your own boss is in it too! Boy, Oh Boy! Wait until the newspapers get hold of this!"

"No," shouted Sammy desperately, in return. "You've got it all wrong ..." He turned to the intercom and interrupted the cardinal, 'Eminence, come in here at once; the police are arresting me on account of what that idiot Father Pongo Black has said – he's in their cells down at the Station ..."

The cardinal's voice came through clearly, its tone a mixture of sadness and resignation.

"I knew it would happen one day, Sammy. Well, I'll write to your mother, don't you worry about that, and of course if you need clean undies, I see to them being sent to you in prison … I'll pray for you as I do for all prisoners; for all those poor misguided ones who have gone astray; who …"

Whatever else the cardinal was going to say was stifled by Sammy grabbing the machine, and throwing it through the plate glass window. He then turned and faced the policeman who was staring at the shattered glass.

"Inspector, you're making a terrible mistake and the cardinal has made it worse; he has a fiendish sense of humour – he doesn't realise this is serious. I'll come with you but I'm warning you: it will all end as some kind of childish joke of that retarded, so-called, friend of mine, Pongo. And, I'm warning you in advance, Inspector, that when I see him at the station, I'm going to give him two of the blackest eyes you've ever seen." He gathered his notebook, his wallet and keys.

"Right, Inspector, let's go … … What are you doing? … There's no need for handcuffs, I give you my word of honour I shall not try to escape … Oh, very well; put them on, if it makes you feel better."

***

The first person Sammy saw in the Charge room was his so-called 'friend', Father Pongo Black. Pongo was dressed as the inspector had said: a full Santa suit complete with whiskers and cap. Being handcuffed, Sammy couldn't do what he would have liked to do, so had to be content with lunging forward and butting his erstwhile friend in the chest with his head, knocking him to the ground.

Pongo pretended to be badly frightened, and squealed for police protection. Burly policemen rapidly pinned Sammy to the wall, and helped the priest on the floor to rise. Actually Pongo was not hurt at all, being stuffed with two large pillows in his middle region which took the force of the blow.

The inspector was delighted. He rushed to the priest who had been attacked: "Sir, do you wish to charge this dangerous man – this Spotels character – with assault. It was an unprovoked assault, and witnessed by several policeman. You could send him up for at least a couple of years." Pongo put on a heroic, saintly expression of sickening piety.

"No, Inspector. I realise how kind it is of you to suggest such a course of action, but my Calling prevents me from following a path of revenge; I must turn the other cheek. You see, I forgive this poor, wretched sinner who has strayed from the straight and … … Look out! He's coming at me again!"

During the scrimmage that followed, Pongo managed to get near to Sammy. He whispered: "The cardinal knows all about it; he'll explain everything. Don't worry, just relax and enjoy the adventure!"

"Adventure, you cretin! You Homo without the Sapiens … you evolutionary product in reverse … you …"

The inspector intervened. "Put this Spotels character in a cell on his own; he's too dangerous to put with the others," he instructed, "and I want a couple to you to go and arrest the Head Santa – have forgotten what his title is – he's part of the syndicate."

"Head Santa," a Constable asked, "what's a Head Santa?"

"Well, Santa means 'holy' – young Costello told me that – that's why that fat Italian singer was always singing about holy Lucia being Santa."

"A woman Santa?" queried another.

"No, you idiot, but if Santa means holy, then the top priest must be called something holy. Perhaps your Santi-ness?"

"That would be something like, 'Your Holiness' then," another reasoned. "I've seen that one on television, but I think he wears white. You said this one wears red …"

"Yes, just like a Santa, so it has to be something like Santa." The inspector made a decision. "Well, let's just stick with 'sir'; you can't go wrong with that. Off you go and be careful, he could be dangerous – he's old, but he's tricky."

Sammy's handcuffs were unlocked, and he was thrust unceremoniously into a cell which was really a cage, and so close to the main office that he could hear all that was being said there.

The inspector was coordinating the arrest of the cardinal from a speaker phone, and the reports of the police on the ground were clearly audible from the cell.

The inspector's voice was raised in anger: "What do you mean you can't find him? Isn't he in his fancy house? Well, alert all squads to be on the lookout for him … What? Say that again! The *press* have just informed you where he is! God help us! …What has the *press* got to do with it? Send out a message to all men: 'be careful'. If the press is covering this we mustn't put one foot wrong – you know what *they're* like … … Ah! You see the cardinal? …

"*Where* did you say you've seen him? … This must be a bad connection, say it again! No! It just isn't possible. You say *he's* now on the roof of the same bank that the other weasel was – before he was arrested? What's he doing? *He's* dressed as a Santa as well! … And, he's doing *WHAT*? … He has one leg over the chimney leading to the vaults! What is happening to this city? Yes, of course you have to get him … What? The Television News team are recording all of this from other high buildings? Well … wait now … be very careful; everything we do will appear on tonight's television news … Let me think for a moment …

"What did you say? A police helicopter is moving in? What a wonderful idea – you can certainly trust our police to have everything under control; they'll most probably have a special services squad hiding in the chopper. Yes, I thought so; they're letting down a ladder … *What!* … They're helping the old idiot to escape! This is beyond belief … he's hanging onto the last three rungs of the ladder, and the chopper has taken off again …What? What's that? … … It flew too close to the top of the Old Men's Refuge and an old bloke has leapt onto the cardinal's leg! … The chopper's moving towards the park carrying both of them! Good Grief! Send a squad there immediately …What! The cardinal shook the man off over the duck pond … badly hurt? … Oh, only muddy, not much water in the pond … send an ambulance anyway – looks good for the press. Where's the damn chopper now? Coming this way? … … You're *joking*! It's settling the old geezer down gently on *our* roof. Well … get up there, you clowns, and arrest him!"

Sammy, sitting tense with fear and dread, listened to the report and prayed fervently for the cardinal: he was an old man – and nuisance that he was, Sammy was very fond of him. His heart had been in his mouth as he saw, in his mind's eye, the terrifying journey of the old man flying through the air at the end of a ladder suspended from a helicopter! His thoughts were interrupted by more talk from the front desk …

"Yes, Sergeant I can hear you perfectly. You're still back at the Bank scene. Yes, that was the right thing to do …What did you say? There's more trouble? What? Two more Santas have entered the main ground-floor doors, their guns drawn, and have locked the doors behind them! Are the press covering this as well? They are! … Curse them! Well, act the gentlemen; treat these gangsters with courtesy – hard as that may be … … They're coming out? Right, be ready! … Are the guns still drawn? They are! *WHAT!* They've put their gun barrels into their mouths? Good grief! … They must be going to commit suicide – you'll have to rush them

– we can't let the press see us just standing still, and letting men kill themselves – looks bad on the front pages …

"Are you ready? *Wait*! What did you say they were doing? *They're eating the gun barrels* – they appear to be made of, *WHAT*? … *Liquorice*? … I think I'm going mad; or the world is … No, Sergeant, just bring them in – they can join the other escapees from the Asylum here."

***

The cardinal was brought down from the roof and appeared in the main office between two policemen. He looked quite happy but decidedly wind-blown. He was a tall, thin man, but now he was a tall and very fat man having several pillows inside his santa suit; his journey through the air had played havoc with his big snowy beard, his wig and his cap – in short, he looked a shocking caricature of himself. He was put in the same cage as Sammy, who rushed to his side.

"Are you all right, Eminence," Sammy began, "I've been so worried about you; I've …"

"Oh, I'm so disappointed, Sammy," the Cardinal interrupted, sorrowfully, "you sound just the same, even with that awful grey prison pallor. I see that prison life has not improved you – I was hoping a good long stint behind bars would do the trick …"

"What do you mean a good long stint? I've only been in here two hours." Sammy started to become suspicious.

"Just a minute, Eminence, just a minute; would you mind just telling me – what the hell's going on?"

"Ssh! Sammy, they're bringing in the last two bank robbers now." Two young priests in their Santa outfits, came past the cardinal's cell, smiling happily as they chewed on the remainder of their guns, and appeared well satisfied, as they made their way to the cell next door to Pongo's. The cardinal was scanning the area of the front office. He suddenly breathed a big sigh of relief. "At last, I thought they were never coming."

As Charles Cardinal York uttered these words, a horde of pressmen came storming in ignoring Inspector Naseby completely, as other policemen let the priests out of their cells. Flash bulbs were going off like Cracker Night, and then the press made way for the Commissioner of Police, who shook hands with the cardinal and Father Pongo Black. Only then did the commissioner acknowledge the presence of the inspector. Aware that all he would say would be on the television news that night, and in the evening papers, the commissioner spoke solemnly, and with careful enunciation:

"Gentlemen, I cannot congratulate you enough for the wonderful work you have done today, on behalf of the Police Welfare Fund. Never in the history of the Fund have we collected such a huge amount of money. It will be used to benefit all those killed, or injured, in the line of duty for their widows and dependents.

"Your Eminence, to you we owe our greatest thanks. To allow yourself to be thought a common bank robber, the ring leader of a robber syndicate, and even to permit us to arrest you, was an act of such generosity that the police will never forget.

"A special word of thanks must go to the other priests involved, especially Father Black, who suggested the whole scheme, and who arranged with the press to cover the entire escapade, and now I'll hand you over to Inspector Naseby."

The cardinal and the priests were standing near their cells, but Sammy was standing next to Naseby. The poor inspector was standing with his mouth gaping wide, in astonishment, and was looking plainly ridiculous! Sammy turned sideways so that the newsmen would not see him, and spoke out of the corner of his mouth:

"Inspector, just repeat the words I tell you."

The policeman nodded, and swallowed. Sammy began to whisper, but it seemed as if the inspector was making his own speech as he repeated the words he heard in his ear.

"Commissioner, Gentlemen of the Clergy and Gentlemen of the Press, this has been a red-letter day in my career on this wonderful Force that we serve. The hardest part for me, and my men, was to keep up the pretence that we thought it was all for real – we tried our very hardest to make it seem real, so as to keep the whole plan secret.

"I want to thank his Santa … I mean, His Eminence … for entering so whole-heartedly into the scheme; he is an elderly man and my heart was in my mouth, when I knew he was dangling on a ladder from a helicopter! However, he's a real trooper and did us proud. And, finally, to all the priests involved, I can only say two very sincere words: *thank you*."

There was vociferous clapping and hand-shaking all around. Only two men refused to shake hands with Pongo: they were the inspector and Sammy.

As the Press men hurried off to make their deadlines, and the police left for other duties, only the cardinal, Pongo, the inspector, and Sammy were left. Sammy addressed the policeman:

"Inspector, I don't think that Father Black's car registration is in order and, if I remember rightly, I think he has been suspended from driving for six months. Would you just check that for me?" The inspector's eyes began to gleam. He rushed off to his computer to do as he was bid.

"Hey, I say, Sammy, old chap," entreated Pongo, "you wouldn't leave a chum to walk home would you?"

"Well, I have no option, of course – we simply can't have you breaking the Law can we? You could catch a bus, but, unfortunately, they're all on strike today, but it's only a ten mile walk; do you good, you know, you're getting quite stout."

The cardinal intervened. "Sammy, the police are going to provide a car for us; surely there's room …"

"No, there isn't," snapped Sammy. "Come on *now*, Eminence, we have a load of work to do back at the Cathedral." He turned, as the grinning Policeman returned.

"Good Afternoon, Inspector, I know we can rely on you to see that Father Black does *not* drive away from here – it's a pity, but he *will* have to walk won't he?"

'He certainly will; I'll see to that. I've arranged for a car to drive you and the cardinal back to the cathedral, and a police-car to shadow Father Black all the way home to see he *does* walk. I mean … we, on the Force, want to do the best we can for the main person responsible for this wonderful day he has given us – a day we will not forget in a hurry, *believe me*."

Sammy shook the policeman's hand. "Inspector Naseby, it's been a real pleasure working with you; you and I understand each other perfectly, don't we."

"We do, Father Spotels," agreed the Inspector fervently, "we certainly *do*!"

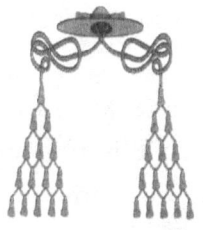

DÉJÀ VU

While most people agreed that Charles Cardinal York – the Archbishop of the city – was, well … *slightly* eccentric, those few persons who had the opportunity to actually *know* him, were also aware that the cardinal had a wickedly, 'child-like' sense of humour. Hidden within his episcopal breast, he had a highly developed sense of the ridiculous, but through severe discipline, restraint and training, he managed to present to the world, a picture of unruffled seriousness and dignity.

However, from time to time the ridiculous came bubbling up, seemingly unstoppable, within the old man, and he sought ways to express this – when he could get away with it – in an unconventional manner.

Thus, when he was notified, by diplomatic post straight from Rome, that his long suffering secretary and master of ceremonies, Father Sammy Spotels, was to be elevated to the hierarchy, the cardinal's first thought was, the *method*, he could use to inform Sammy – of whom he had grown fond over the years they had been together – in an amusing and unusual manner.

The letter from Rome informed the cardinal, the announcement had to be kept 'in petto' until a certain date, ten days hence. Only then, would the cardinal be free to inform Father Spotels of his promotion, and inform the press that his secretary was to receive a mitre.

This gave the cardinal a leeway of ten days, to decide on his plan. His mind ranged over a 'Blimp' flying through the air, trailing a huge message behind it. Or, perhaps, a surprise raid from the Terrorist Squad on Sammy – he could give them a fake 'tip-off', and they could use it as a practice exercise. Or, perhaps, a funny cartoon in the National newspapers with Sammy struggling – with his prize-fighter's face, and in his boxing gear – to pull off a 'too-tight' mitre.

None of the ideas really pleased Charles. He went for a walk around his beloved city, and looked for inspiration into shop windows. This was unproductive, until he reached a certain window which only featured a beautifully presented sign, together with a large picture of a *Gorilla*.

The cardinal stopped dead in his tracks. A 'Gorilla-gram' – the very thing! Charles peered at the sign, but was exasperated to discover he had left his reading glasses at home! He couldn't read the print without them. However, that wasn't going to stop him now he had the idea. He entered the shop and said simply: "I want one. I don't care what it costs, but I want one; it must be delivered on the 20th of this month."

The two people behind the desk, staring into their computers, looked up at their customer in amazement. They recognized him immediately – he had been in the city forever.

They were surprised at this request from a cardinal of the Church, but if he could pay for it; that really was all that mattered – they thought it was all a pretty silly advertising gimmick anyhow.

They mentioned the price to the cardinal, and he blinked. He had no idea these messages cost so much. He hesitated a moment, but then decided that Sammy deserved it – he had been a good, faithful and, indeed kindly, colleague – so he agreed to the price.

The cardinal then informed the people when the 'Gorilla' was to arrive, and what message it had to bring. This puzzled the Zoo reps. *Message*, they queried? He wanted a *message*? ... However, after some confusion, they, being kindly people, finally agreed to have a sign printed. The wording of the sign puzzled them even more – it didn't make sense! It read: 'Bumps a daisy, lad, you've struck the Jackpot!'

The days seem to crawl slowly towards the 'big day'. The cardinal was unusually tetchy, and hard to please; it was also difficult for his secretary to get his boss to concentrate for long, on any of a dozen, different important engagement details that had to be worked out.

At last the ten days were up; the waiting was over. Both the cardinal and his secretary went to their respective offices at 8.30 in the morning, to begin their normal routine.

However, it was *not quite* routine, for the cardinal had snuck into Father Spotel's office earlier, and pushed down the switch on the intercom, that enabled him to hear from that office, and also from the front office, where the two ladies worked. He had also put on his head – for this festive occasion – his beloved 'Father Brown' Roman hat. He knew Sammy hated it!

As the time approached nine o'clock, the cardinal stopped work and sat, smiling, as he listened to the shuffling of papers, and quiet exclamations from his secretary, as Sammy worked on the newspapers as per usual.

While waiting, the cardinal's imagination took flight. He chuckled as he imagined what would happen if a mistake were made, and they sent a *real* gorilla instead of a 'pretend' one.

Charles was a very old man, and he drifted off into, what he thought, was a little doze, with his mind actively working overtime.

He thought he was dreaming when he actually heard the panic in the front office, with Miss Wright and Miss Nubbs screaming at their first sight of the gorilla.

He heard their frantic cries for help to Father Sammy … then suddenly – to his horror – he actually heard Sammy shouting that he was *going to shoot the monster with his hunting rifle!* The cardinal sat up straight, now wide-awake with the fearful awareness: *this was no dream*!

A sudden terrifying realisation brought him to his feet: *only he could save the life of the innocent MAN in the gorilla suit* – apparently everyone else thought it was a real gorilla!

Charles leapt from his desk, rushed into Sammy's office, and threw himself in front of the beast just as poor Sammy pulled the trigger. The cardinal fell to the ground with a gigantic hole blasted in his 'Father Brown' hat. Sammy gazed, stupefied, at the sight of his superior lying – as he thought – dead, at the feet of the gorilla, and fainted.

Pandemonium then ensued as the Police, the Fire Brigade and Zoo attendants – summonsed by the ever-efficient Miss Wright – charged into the small office. The noise was hideous as the women redoubled their screaming, at the sight of the dead cardinal.

As Charles slowly regained consciousness, he looked up through the hole in his hat which had fallen across his face, and imagined he could see a *real* gorilla bending over him. I must be worse than I thought, he reasoned; such a thing was impossible! When the beast's saliva dripped onto his face from the massive jaws, Charles understood that the impossible had become all too possibly, possible. There was only one thing to do, so he did it – he fainted.

***

An hour later, the cardinal sat beside the couch on which lay a white-faced Father Spotels.

"You're not dead? Truly?' Sammy asked tremulously.

"Not on your life; never felt better, *my Lord Bishop*," the cardinal answered jovially.

"There's no need to be frivolous," Sammy declared querulously. "It was no joking matter I tell you. I very nearly killed you."

"Well, how was I to know that they would send a real gorilla! You'd think they would've had more sense! But, enough of that; I've explained that it was all a misunderstanding; they've all gone home, and taken the nasty beast with them. Now, about the important thing, my Lord."

"What gives with this, 'My Lord', business?" Sammy asked. "Is this another one of your ridiculous pranks?"

"No, you silly chump! I'm trying to tell you something. You are to be the new auxiliary Bishop Samuel Spotels, of the titular Church of Darumbuljka."

Sammy sat upright. Could this be another of the cardinal's jokes?

"Eminence," he stuttered agitatedly, "is that *really* the truth? … And, where the hell is Darumbuljka? Is it a residential See?"

"No, it's not …" answered the cardinal, then murmured, mischievously, "more's the pity …"

"What did you say?" demanded Sammy sharply.

"I said: It's *itty-bitty* – the place – I mean."

"But, it can't be true," spluttered Sammy.

The Cardinal looked surprised. "Of course it's true! That's what the message was all about."

"*Message?*" quavered Sammy. "There was no message; I didn't see any message."

"Well, how *could* you, you silly boy! You acted just like King David … *you shot the messenger!*"

LOVE THROUGH
A GLASS DARKLY

It was the written complaint from the French cardinal that first suggested the rumour.

Charles, Cardinal York read, with dismay, the details of the outraged cardinal. The French prelate had been their guest, too, which made it worse! He had only been here for a few days, and for this to happen! It wouldn't end here, Charles knew; soon everyone would be talking about it – now that Sammy was a bishop.

Charles sighed. He really was too old to have to cope with all these problems with the clergy now. Besides that, it didn't make sense! He knew, or *thought* he knew, his one-time secretary, Father Sammy Spotels, through and through, and such a suggestion was not only libellous – it was downright ridiculous.

He couldn't believe that Sammy, his trusted companion and colleague, was living a double life. Trust the French, he thought mutinously, to dig up the dirt! Immediately after *that* thought, Charles was aware how wrong it was, and begged God to forgive him.

The French cardinal was only doing his duty, Charles thought with dismay, but heaven help us if he is correct! I really don't know what I'm going to do.

There's nothing for it, Charles decided. I'll have to call Sammy in. There's no use in just sitting here worrying, when I really don't understand it at all. The old cardinal's face suddenly lightened. Perhaps, after all, it could be that Sammy has a perfectly logical explanation, and all this is a mountain made from a mole hill.

Charles lifted the receiver and was immediately answered by his new secretary – an unpleasant, unsmiling, young supercilious priest, called Father Biderbacher – the cardinal detested him! He forced himself to be icily polite.

"Eminence?"

"Father, can you tell me if his Lordship, Samuel Spotels, is still in the building?"

"He is, your Eminence; is it your wish to converse with him?"

"Please. Would you kindly ascertain whether he is free to attend me as soon as possible?"

"It shall be done, Eminence, expeditiously."

Charles sighed again. I think I'll burst something if I have to continue being so damned polite every time I speak to that ghastly chap. Why can't he say 'talk with him' instead of always 'converse'? I'd like never to have to 'converse' with him about anything; and, whoever uses a word like *expeditiously*? I'd like to throw something *expeditiously* at him! I'd like …

His musings were interrupted by a heavy thump on his office door. It opened, and Bishop Samuel Spotels clumped into the room.

"Okey-dokey, Eminence, what's the big flap?" he asked breezily, and sat down, uninvited, in an easy chair in front of the cardinal's desk. "I've just been talking to that new chap – a proper jerk isn't he? Perhaps he'll improve in time. Don't let him push you around." The young bishop paused, and studied the old cardinal closely. His jocose manner changed.

"What *is* the matter, Eminence," he asked gently. "I'm sorry I was jocular; I can see it's serious. Tell me about it; perhaps I can help. Who's been making a heap of trouble for you, this time?"

"*You!*" answered the cardinal abruptly, then his voice softened: "Sammy, how could you? After all the years we've been jogging along together? You've put up with me and I've put up with you – even tolerating your wretched motorbike – and I honestly thought, of all the priests that I have to be responsible for, I could count on you with all my being. And, now I find that I have been deceived! Oh, Sammy, Sammy, Sammy!"

"For the love of heaven, stop your 'O Sammy' litany, and tell me what the hell I'm supposed to have done."

"Not supposed, Sammy," responded the cardinal holding up the letter from France, "I have proof."

"Let me see that," demanded the young Bishop. "Oh, it's from that French cardinal – a proper pain in the butt he was! I remember you saying the same thing, when he was staying with us, didn't you?"

"That's enough of that, my Lord Bishop," the cardinal answered severely. "Whether we happened to actually like the French prelate, or not, is irrelevant. He has issued a complaint against you."

"He has issued *what*?"

"A complaint."

"Why, the ungrateful, slimy wretch. I was run ragged driving him all over the city the few days he was here; he wanted to see everything. There was only one night I had off to try and get my own work done, when I sent him off on his own, in the official car, with Joe driving him."

"Apparently, *that night* was the problem."

"Oh, why?"

"Well, he claims that he told you specifically that he wanted to attend the evening Solemn Vespers at the Ruthenian-Rite

Cathedral, as their special guest, and you sent him, by Episcopal car, to our version of the Folies Bergère."

"*What!*"

"Exactly! He claims that he was never so insulted in all his life; that he had to stand outside the 'wicked house of ill repute' – his own words – for one full hour waiting for the car to return, in his full Episcopal regalia."

"Good God!"

"Indeed, and worse still," continued the cardinal, "he said that people thought he was busking, dressed up as he was, and threw small change at his feet."

"No!" Sammy started to laugh at the mental picture forming in his mind, only to be silenced by a stern warning from the cardinal.

"Look!" declared Sammy. "It's the silly chap's own fault. He insisted on speaking French all the time he was here, although he could speak English perfectly. He most probably gave instructions in French to poor old Joe the driver – who doesn't speak French at all – and refused to correct him in English. My own French is not crash-hot, I know, but I managed to get by with him – but Joe! Why he wouldn't have understood a word the Frenchman said to him. As I said, it's the clown's own fault, the silly twit!" Sammy paused. "If that's all there is then…"

"There's more to come, my Lord," Charles added. "The French cardinal claims that only a man *in love* could have been so stupid, as to have done such a thing and demands that I examine you carefully, as to whether that is the case or not. He has threatened to write to Rome if I do not."

"You're joking!"

"Would to God I were. Now, my Lord Bishop – no more joking please – this is serious. Look at me, Sammy. I want you to tell me honestly, considering all we have been through together, is there a female in your life?"

Sammy hung his head, and sighed. "Eminence, I'm sorry it has come to this. You know I'd never lie to you, so I'll tell you the truth: yes, there is. I'm sorry, but that *is* the case."

"Oh, dear Lord, Sammy! What possessed you? You have such a great career ahead of you …"

"I suppose, Eminence, that being just an ordinary man like all others, I was looking for some love and companionship …"

"But why didn't you tell me immediately? We've been friends a long time; I could have helped. We could have talked it over together."

"I suppose I was secretly hoping you wouldn't find out."

"So the sin is compounded with *deceit*. Oh, Sammy, how could you let me down in this way? Tell me quickly about this female. Is it a young woman?"

"Well, she's pretty young, but she's definitely not a minor. I've never asked her age, it wouldn't be polite."

"Very beautiful?"

"Absolutely, or at least I think so, although others may not think the same. Every time I see her, I feel my heart soars. I feel I am close to heaven itself."

"Careful, son, that's close to heresy."

"She's not perfect, I know. She has a weight problem, but then I've never liked those skeleton-model-type females myself. I think she must dye her hair; it is a strange blue-grey colour, but very beautiful." Bishop Spotels looked earnestly at his superior.

"I just don't deserve her. Look at me: a crooked nose and a cauliflower ear, through all those hours in the boxing ring at University. I'm hardly a beauty, so why she should choose me is beyond me – it is a mystery that she should ever love me."

The cardinal shuddered, and closed his eyes; his worst fears realised. The young bishop was not even remorseful! He opened his eyes again and continued gravely with the questioning:

"Tell me, how long has this obsession been going on?"

"Oh, only about six months, I think it is."

"Good, then it won't take much will power on your part to stop it immediately."

"*Stop* it?"

"Oh course, you *must* stop it. You are a priest, and not only a priest, but a *bishop*! Think of the scandal you are giving. If this Frenchie knows about it, then very soon others will obviously know as well."

"I suppose you're right. I've kept it pretty much a secret, but it's out in the open now, I know. You see, she came with me today to the office."

"She *never did*!" shouted the cardinal. "The brazen hussy! Have you taken leave of your senses? Are you completely without shame? You have taken solemn vows to God and you regard them as nothing?" The cardinal paused for breath. "Dear God, is nothing sacred with you anymore? I never dreamed this would happen; I should have prevented your consecration as bishop; you'll have to be defrocked. Oh, Lord, Lord, Lord God, forgive this wretched man! Oh, the shame of it all!"

Bishop Spotels asked the cardinal, his face puckered with concern: "Would you like to meet the lady, Eminence?"

The cardinal grimaced. "I most definitely would *NOT like* to meet her but I suppose I *must*. Perhaps I can talk some sense into *her*. Tell me, what is her name?"

"I'll only tell you her first name. It's Delilah."

"Seems appropriate! So, like her namesake, she seduced you."

"She certainly did. Completely bowled over I was; it was love at first sight; I felt woozy in the head when I saw her; I thought my feet had left the ground and I was floating like a cloud; I saw flowers all around me ...There was music playing in the trees ... I ..."

"Stop that nauseating bilge! That's quite enough; it's straight out of one of those dreadful celebrity magazines," shouted the cardinal, "I've had enough of this! Bring the wretched trollop in!"

Bishop Samuel Spotels turned his head to the door and called: "Come in Delilah dear; it's all right, the cardinal will see you."

The room exploded into sound as the door crashed open on its hinges, and in bounded a huge, young St Bernard dog, its long blue-grey hair flowing as its gigantic feet crashed on the wooden floor then slid on the carpet square. The dog paused, bared its teeth at the cardinal, then seeing its master, nearly flattened him by jumping onto his lap and kissing him with its huge red tongue. Sammy disappeared from sight under the size and weight of the huge dog.

Sammy struggled back into an upright position and holding the dog tightly by the collar, looked at the cardinal. Shaking with suppressed laughter, and trying desperately to keep a straight face, he said: "Eminence, may I present to you Miss Delilah Spotels."

The cardinal, who usually was never at a loss for words, goggled at the spectacle before him. Realizing he had been tricked once again, he picked up the vase of flowers on his desk; threw it at both man and dog, as he shouted: "Get out! Get out! *Get out!*"

It was only when Bishop Spotels and his dog were leaving the room – both covered with water and blooms – that the old man started to laugh helplessly, tears running down his cheek.

Sammy, closing the door, heard the old man say: "Oh, Sammy, Sammy, why aren't you still here with us? Nothing's the same since you were made a bishop and taken away from us. Everyday something funny used to happen."

Alone in his office once more, Charles looked down on his

desk, and saw the letter that had caused all the trouble. I'll deal with that mischief-making Frenchman – cardinal or not – in a letter he won't forget in a hurry, he decided. And I'll send him a photo of Father Spotels' *lover*.

That'll take the smirk off his sanctimonious face!

EPISCOPAL FLUTTERS
IN THE OLD DART
(THE CARDINAL TAKES ON ENGLAND)

His Eminence Charles Cardinal York and His Lordship Bishop Samuel Spotels – the cardinal's one-time secretary; now the Titular Bishop of Darumbuljka – were sitting together in the airport terminal waiting for their plane to be called. The younger bishop, for some reason, was holding on to the edge of the older man's black suit-coat.

The cardinal had now reached the age of seventy-five, and had been invited to Rome to receive permission to retire, in person, from the pope himself; they were old friends. The cardinal had invited Bishop Spotels to accompany him on the long journey, as a friend, and also, he thought shrewdly, in case anything went wrong.

Bishop Spotels was grateful for the company of his old friend, and one-time boss, as he needed to go to Rome himself to consult the curial offices regarding the restoration of his new diocese to a residential See, so both friends were happy they could travel together.

In their travel plans, the two prelates intended to make a brief visit to an old friend of the cardinal's in London; then, go on to

Rome. They both thought it would be wise to travel to London first; the elderly cardinal could rest up for a couple of days after the long flight.

The younger bishop, usually called 'Sammy' by the cardinal, was a stocky, muscular man with a battered, humorous face and crew-cut hair. He was beginning to get tense, and kept his eyes fixed firmly on his companion.

The cardinal was tall and ascetic-looking, closely resembling a particularly fragile saint from a stained-glass window – which was a joke, Sammy thought; the old chap was as tough as an old boot!

Sammy knew the danger period was beginning as the time of departure drew ever closer; he knew well how awkward things could become if he didn't watch the devious cardinal like a hawk. He was therefore ready when the old man stood up suddenly to ask his next question, Sammy's hand grasped, even more firmly, onto the tail of the cardinal's coat.

"Are you absolutely sure, Sammy, that we've got everything? We'll be away for several weeks you know. I can't remember whether we left the budgerigar with Rising Damp, or not."

"Eminence, I'm not going to answer that question again, and that's that; there's no use asking," Bishop Samuel Spotels answered brusquely, then added: "And, you know perfectly well, the housekeeper is *not* called 'Rising Damp' …"

"Well she always *seems* so damp; she's always *washing* things. Last time it was the toaster – it's never worked since. I tried to fix it with a fork, but it gave me a tremendous shock; I don't use it any more … But, Rising Damp … she might decide to wash poor Percival; he could drown, poor little chap … However," the cardinal admitted, genuinely contrite. "You're right, of course; I did ask that before, but you know, Sammy, how tense I get waiting in these awful places – all glass, dribbling children, and raucous announcements." The cardinal went to move away. "I think I'll just wander around for a little; that might help me relax…"

"Oh, no you don't! Not on your life," Sammy answered sharply, pulling the cardinal back down again firmly by his coat. "Remember the last time when you just 'wandered' off; you ended up in Moscow, and what a job I had to find you and get you back here again."

"It was a very interesting experience," the cardinal protested indignantly. "I met the Russian Orthodox Metropolitan …"

"And the Chief of Police."

"Yes … but look at the positive side; I learned Russian."

"Oh, yes? You *could* say that, only if the Russian language consists of just two words: 'Da' and 'Nyet'. You used 'Nyet' so often they ended up calling you the 'Metropolitan Nyet' in the prison."

"Where the food was terrible! I tell you what, Sammy," the cardinal lowered his voice, and advised the bishop confidentially, his face serious, "if you're ever going to turn to crime, then don't go to Russia. You'd die if you had to live on …"

"Ssh. Ssh! They're calling our plane. So now, Eminence, just pick up your hand luggage, then it's just in through the metal detector, for a final check, and we'll be off. The plane will be leaving in about 30 minutes."

The two clergymen joined the queue, and Bishop Spotels began praying silently to St Jude; travelling with the cardinal, one needed all the help one could get!

***

Sammy sighed as he tried to find room for his legs. He knew the cardinal's decision to always fly economy was motivated by a desire to travel as cheaply as other ordinary people did, but being human, Sammy often wished that, just occasionally, the cardinal would overcome his scruples, and try business class instead.

For one thing, the food … His thoughts were interrupted by his elderly companion.

"Do you know, Sammy, that although this food tastes exactly as though it were made of plastic, it is said to be very healthy and good for you?"

"Oh, yes? Where exactly did your read that? An airline booklet by any chance?"

"Well, yes it was, but it's not too bad, really. The reason I'm not eating anything is that I am determined to lose this excess weight. It has worried me for some time now."

"Really? Just where is this excess weight located? You're as thin as a beanpole and always have been… whereas I actually *do* need to diet. Somehow or other, I have put on ten kilos over my boxing weight. I'm determined to get that off."

"Yes, I've noticed, Sammy. You really need to diet; so you see, all things do work out for the best, don't they? You can't eat this food; you'll take off several pounds – I don't like those kilo things – and soon you'll be prancing around again like a youngster."

"I said I wanted to lose weight; I didn't say I wanted to starve to death …"

"Not another word about it; we're travelling like all our flock and that's that."

"Next time, I'll travel for the first time in my life, as one of the *wealthy* members of *my* flock."

The cardinal refused to be drawn, so pretended not to hear. He wondered what he could do to cope with the deadly boredom of sitting, for so long, in a cramped position.

His eye lighted on the 'emergency situations' pamphlet; this was just what the passengers would enjoy. He used his big strong voice, and began reading from the card he was holding. It detailed just about every catastrophe that could ever possibly happen while travelling by air – for the edification of the other passengers.

Two young nervous women in the seat across the aisle, listening to the cardinal, became terrified, and started to cry with fright – the flight attendant rushed to their assistance. After cleverly dealing with the girls, the grim-faced flight attendant snatched the emergency pamphlet from the hands of the cardinal without a word.

Sammy immediately put on earphones, opened his breviary and began to say his Office; he was not going to say one word in defence of the cardinal this time.

Sammy had learned through the many years he had been with the cardinal, to concentrate on what he was doing himself, or he would never finish anything, so he said his office slowly, and thoughtfully, relishing the beauty of the ancient, timeless psalms.

***

The next hour passed without incident; their flight was smooth and the gentle hum had made the two bishops sleepy. Already the cardinal's head was nodding. They had discussed the upcoming visits with the Holy Father; Sammy's special briefing on his imminent move to the newly-restored Diocese of Darumbuljka that he would get from the boffins in the curial offices in the Vatican, and both men were carefully avoiding the one topic that was in the minds of both: Sammy impending departure, both from his home country, and from his old friend with whom he had been for fifteen years – firstly, as his secretary and master of ceremonies, and then as his auxiliary bishop.

Now they were to go their separate ways, and Sammy was worried about the old man. He had never hinted at his plans for retirement. Where would he go, he wondered, and what would he do?

Sammy made a sudden decision; he would ask the cardinal

straight out, no more mincing words.

"Eminence, I was wondering ..."

"Um? Yes?"

"What exactly do you intend *doing* in retirement? I mean do you have any family left that you would like to live with?"

"I do have a younger sister, Sammy. But her husband and I have never got on. It didn't help that my sister married an atheist, of course, but I have to admit he's been a good husband to her, and to the seven kids. But, it's his attitude to me, that's the difficulty ...You see, he doesn't like me; he once said he'd like to shoot me."

"Good Heavens! Why was that?

"Well, he's never really forgiven me."

"Goodness gracious! What for?"

"Well, I find it hard to understand myself, but just because I burnt down their house, you wouldn't think ..."

"You *What*?"

"Sssh! don't carry on about it! How was *I* to know that if I mixed the two chemicals together they would explode?"

"*You* mixed chemicals together? What the hell were you doing?"

"Young Danny, the eldest boy, wanted help with his homework one day when I was visiting, and Adolph ..."

"*Adolph*?"

"Well, that's what I called him – the husband; his real name was Cecil. Anyhow, Cecil was being sarcastic when he said that I was supposed to be a great scholar – wasting my life all those years at university, studying – and I couldn't even help a sixteen year old boy with his homework. So ... I thought I'd have to show him ..."

"But you've never studied Chemistry, or general Science?"

"I realised that when the house blew up."

"Dear God! No wonder they don't want you for a guest! Was anyone killed, or badly hurt."

"No ... only Danny ..."

"How can you say '*only* Danny'? That's terrible. What happened to him?"

"He had just started to shave, and had a little stubble of beard on his chin that he was intensely proud of; in the explosion, it burnt right off. He never forgave me. Even when he became a Bishop, and we meet at posh conferences, we just bow politely to each other."

"He's a *Bishop*?"

"Oh course, he's a bishop. I just don't talk about him, and he doesn't talk about me either, that's all."

"And all because of a scrubby bit of beard."

"Well ... there *were* a few other things. You see, I accidentally poisoned his little dog, as well. It was one of those *tiny* dogs; looked like a rat." The cardinal looked irritated. "Now, there's no need for you to look at me like that. It was not intentional."

"Give me strength! What did you do?"

"Well, Hercules was off colour, and I was trying to cure the wretched animal by natural methods. I had read this old Victorian book on remedies for *horses*, and I thought it should work on *dogs* as well. You see, if you mix ..."

"*Spare me, Eminence,* I can bear no more. Just go to sleep will you ..."

The cardinal smiled; he thought that would shut Sammy up. He looked fondly at the younger man; good old Sammy, he thought, he'd believe anything!

Sammy yawned. "Well, Eminence, we'll have to think up something, less dangerous, for you to do in your retirement. Oh, dear! I can't keep awake. Why don't you just tilt your seat back a little, stretch out those long legs of yours and see if you can nod off?"

"Good idea, Sammy. I really am very tired ... really tired; it's been a long and tiring year … so much work … so many ceremonies ….But, I'm looking forward to London…so restful …"

The men slept.

***

Arriving in London on a miserable grey and bleak day, the cardinal and bishop shivered as they left the plane. Charles thought the rude remark made by the flight attendant as they left the plane door, totally uncalled for. She had suggested to them that they might consider using another airline next time they travelled! The nerve of her! He determined to write to the management.

The two men collected their luggage, and Sammy carefully piled all their belonging onto a trolley. They then waited outside the terminal for the car which would take them to stay with the cardinal's old friend, an elderly bishop living in the East End.

Eventually, a tall middle-aged, corpulent Indian gentleman arrived in a very small black car and collected both prelates and their luggage. He introduced himself as Thomas, and announced that he was the driver, and chief cook, at the bishop's house.

With great difficulty Thomas, aided by Sammy, succeeded in tying most of their luggage onto the roof-rack, and the rest was piled onto the passengers' laps as they squeezed into the back seat.

The two bishops, peering over the top of cases, professed themselves delighted to meet the Indian, while the cardinal whispered to Sammy: "We'll have curry each meal, just wait and see." Both he and Sammy were united in their detestation of curry.

Charles then answered a question from the driver, "You're so right, Thomas, a lovely day indeed; it's so … so very … bracing!" Charles whispered aside to Sammy, "I'm freezing to death; how can anyone live in this climate. I should've put on another sweater."

They soon arrived at the English bishop's house in Mulberry

Street. It was a poor street with terrace houses running to seed, uncared-for front gardens, tattooed youths were lounging against walls, cigarettes hanging from the edge of their lips. There seemed a positive fetish for metal pieces of all shapes being inserted into faces, necks, and arms, for ornamentation. There was a rather high smell from uncollected garbage bins pervading the area.

The cardinal was surprised that this would be where the bishop's house was located, and he noted with alarm that there was a high wall around the large, old building where the bishop lived, with barbed wire on the top. He nudged Sammy and pointed to the wire.

Turning again to the driver, he asked. "Thomas is there much crime in this area of London?"

"Oh yes, sir. We have much crime, very, very much crime. We very famous, for crime here."

"Famous for crime? Really? Oh well, I suppose that's the case everywhere now. The house would be safe enough though, wouldn't it?"

"Goodness gracious me, no, Your Eminence," replied Thomas. "We have many 'in-breaks'." Thomas, belatedly, realised he was alarming the guests, so hastened to add. "But, not to worry, Excellency, I sleep on cot inside front door with rifle. I very good shot; yes sir, very good shot, indeed."

"I see. It's certainly reassuring to hear that, Thomas." Charles shuddered. "Would you arrange a cot inside the *back* door as well? Bishop Spotels will sleep there during our time in London."

Sammy sat up. "Hey, just a minute …"

"Not another word, Sammy, that's the end of the matter … Look, there's dear old Bishop Francis Appleton standing out in the street to welcome us. Oh, dear old Frankie; he must be a hundred; I know he's older than I am. How is he coping with the cold in this dreadful climate? He must be freezing! When we get out Sammy, give him your overcoat until we get him inside and before a fire – there *must* be a fire."

The car stopped neatly outside the house, and the cardinal jumped out, cases flying everywhere, and took the very old bishop in his arms and hugged him. He then introduced Sammy who did offer his coat to the bishop, but was refused. "Thank you, my boy; it's very kind of you, but I have no need for it on such a lovely day as this."

Sammy realised that he'd better be careful of what he said about the weather while he was staying at this house.

***

In fact, the house was delightfully warm and soon the three men were sitting in front of a small fire with a cup of good coffee made by the multi-tasking Thomas. The talk tended to be of church matters; of the cardinal's upcoming visit to the Holy Father in Rome, and then of the surprising re-establishment of the Diocese of Darumbuljka.

The very old English bishop was a learned, and courteous man, and soon they were all chatting freely. He explained that he had been permitted to retire and live in his old house, while a young Monsignor and two curates lived closer to the small cathedral, and did all the work. They were good men, the bishop said, and he was quite happy here with just dear old Thomas, his driver, and an old lady who came in to care for the house and do the laundry.

He rarely had visitors, and for that reason, he had been looking forward so much to this visit of his old friend, Charles, and … he smiled kindly at Sammy … at the young 'boy bishop' as he persisted in calling him; which amused Sammy greatly.

The cardinal asked about the security problem. The bishop nodded sadly. Yes, it was a terrible problem; nearly every house in the street had either been robbed or vandalised. He expressed his gratitude to Thomas for his constant and faithful vigilance and protection.

It was, unfortunately, a very rough area, but the bishop said he was used to it and loved it. He had been offered a better place to live, but had chosen to remain here where he had been for so long now. Charles was a very understanding man; he saw that the disparaging talk of the area was distressing to the old man, so rapidly changed the subject to His Lordship's Cathedral. The old man brightened at once.

"When you have rested you must come and see it. It's not a great, huge Cathedral your Eminence, but we think it is beautiful; and I think the people do too. They might be poor people here, but they are very good, and kind people, on the whole."

"We'd be delighted to see it, Frankie, wouldn't we, Sammy?"

"Well, I certainly would, my Lord Bishop," Sammy replied sincerely. He stood up, "with your permission, both the cardinal and I would be privileged to be able to offer Holy Mass there tomorrow morning. But now, by your leave, I'm going to shoot off and try to see an old friend of mine, who has been doing some study at Oxford. He's a cleric as well."

"Oh, that's quite a long way from here. You must eat first. I've asked Thomas, for your very first meal as my guests, to make a really special, authentic curry; you'll love it – it's so hot you'll think you are actually in India itself." The old man chuckled wheezily.

Both men closed their eyes tightly for a moment, but the cardinal recovered first. He smiled gently. "I can hardly wait, Frankie, and I know how much Sammy is looking forward to it." Sammy, sitting to the left of the old man, shuddered. He had hoped the excuse of meeting an old friend would have excused him from eating anything at all. However, there being no escape, he faced the inevitable.

"I'm famished," he lied, smiling valiantly.

***

The weather on the travellers' first night in London turned very cold, but fine; a clear moon shed its radiance on all the chimney tops in Mulberry Street. Sammy was trying to settle on his uncomfortable, unyielding, portable bed stretched across the inside of the back door of the house.

He was actually shivering with the cold. At last he could bear it no longer, so getting out of bed, he put on a sweater over his pyjamas, and then added socks to his feet. Gradually, after a little time, grumpily trying to find the most comfortable way to lie on the hard bed, he began to nod off; it had been a long and tiring day... After what seemed an eternity, he slept.

Thomas, lying at his post at the front door, usually slept like the dead most nights, but this night he was alert for any unusual sounds in the house.

He was anxious; fully aware of the importance of his guests, and fearful that the local vandals might choose this night to smash a window, or commit some other outrage. He held his rifle in his hands tightly, but then, slowly as the hours passed, he began to relax; the rifle slipped gently to the floor, and the whole house slept.

The cardinal was wakened suddenly by a strange sound. It sounded like footsteps that went quickly past his door. He was out of bed in an instant, and grabbing a walking stick with a large knob on the end of it, in his hand – having appropriated it when he found it in the hallway last evening – he crept to the door and, slowly opening it, listened intently. Yes, there definitely was someone about. He turned the walking stick upside down so that the knob would act as a club.

Before he made a move, he looked at the luminous dial of his watch. It was three o'clock in the morning. He hesitated a moment, troubled; searching at this hour might be embarrassing; it could be someone going to the bathroom – after all, the English bishop was a very old man – but just as he stood there dithering, there was another sound which seemed to come from the main stairs. He decided he had to investigate.

Gripping his weapon tightly, he made his way quietly to the staircase.

It was not completely dark; there was a faint glimmer of moon-light from a sky-light high up in the ceiling. In the misty gloom, the cardinal could vaguely see a figure moving suspiciously. It seemed to be going slowly in and out of the rooms leading from the hall.

The stealthy figure approached the stairs, and the cardinal, firmly holding his club, began to descend the stairs slowly, silently, tread by tread.

Sammy woke with a start. He was not sure, for a moment, just where he was. He went to move in his dreadful bed, but a sharp pain in his hip suddenly reminded him with a vengeance where he was.

He sat up; something had woken him, but what was it? Was there an unusual sound? He listened intently. Yes, someone was moving about; it came from the front area of the house, possibly near the stairs; yes, definitely sounds of movement. Perhaps all those things Thomas had hinted about vandals were true.

Well, Sammy decided, throwing his legs over the side of his

cot, they had chosen the wrong night for it, if they had; he'd teach these English thugs and hooligans a lesson they wouldn't forget in a hurry.

He silently got up from his bed, flexed his shoulders, adopting his boxer stance, then on stockinged feet, made his way to where the noise seemed to have originated.

The old English Bishop was also having a bad night. He always slept lightly, but tonight, for some reason, the house seemed full of strange noises. Please God, he prayed, don't let the vandals attack tonight.

Even though his neighbours were villains, the old man didn't want the cardinal to think badly of them. He listened, holding his hand to his ear, and the noise that had disturbed him, came again. He sighed wearily; he'd have to deal with them once again.

The old man got out of bed, shivering slightly, and putting on his dressing gown, crept out to the landing. He began groping for the main light switch which would light up the entire ground floor. Just as his fingers flipped the switch … …

The cardinal saw in the dim light the head of the intruder in front of him; unfortunately, the intruder at the same moment saw, what *he* thought was an intruder. They lashed out at each other simultaneously. The cardinal was thrown backward, receiving a strong blow from a fist to his left eye, but he wasn't done yet.

In falling backwards, his right arm came round strongly in a circle and, shouting loudly, he struck out at the head before him. There was the sickening sound of a dreadful crack on the side of the man's skull.

The lights now blazing, Sammy rushed to the sound of the shouting, ready to belt the villains senseless, when he stopped dead. He saw the cardinal lying on the stairs, Thomas lying unconscious on the floor, while the old bishop was standing at the top of the stairs, screaming in horror: "Thomas! You've killed Thomas! Oh, my God you've killed him."

Sammy, suddenly realising what the old bishop was about to do, cried out loudly, **"NO! NO! DON'T!"** But, it was too late. The old man rushing to his friend's aid, forgot he was at the top of a flight of stairs, and, stepping into space, went tumbling down, head over heels, to the bottom. He lost consciousness – it appeared that his leg had been broken in the fall – it was twisted strangely beneath him.

The cardinal struggled to his feet and surveyed the carnage through his one good eye – the other was already swelling and blood-red.

Still holding the club, he looked humbly at Sammy.

"I think we'll need an ambulance, Sammy."

As he knelt at the side of the old bishop Sammy felt the Indian stirring, so was relieved to know that, at least, one of the wounded, was not too badly injured. Then, as he gave the cardinal an exasperated look, he fumbled with the unfamiliar emergency number on his cell phone, saying dryly: "Well, they'll certainly remember our visit, won't they? Is there anyone else in the house we could belt up? What about the old woman? …Hello … yes please, I need an ambulance and quickly please, yes three wounded …"

***

Cardinal York and Bishop Spotels left London much earlier than they had intended.

As it turned out, one of the para-medics had a daughter who worked as a reporter on the News of the World newspaper. As a proud dad, he just couldn't resist phoning her, and sending her the photos he took at the scene of the disaster, on his mobile.

Consequently, the shambles of the evening fiasco was splashed all over the front pages of the daily tabloid press the next morning, together with photos.

The headlines screamed: 'Massacre on Mulberry Street'; 'Catholic Cardinal sees Red'; and the most insulting of all: 'Colonial Prelates Pulverise Pensioners'. The photos were terrible. There was one of the cardinal with one eye closed and swollen, still brandishing his club standing over the bodies of Thomas and of the old Bishop, lying at the foot of the stairs, and a highly unflattering one of Sammy looking belligerent, crouched like a boxer, in his short pyjamas and socks.

He looked like an out of work derelict from the underworld.

Not only were the two travellers now 'infamous' but were the target of reporters who thronged the street near the front gate. The infuriated Monsignor, hastily summonsed, had had to bring in a new security firm to cope with the situation and he suggested, with thinly disguised fury, that it might be wise for Cardinal York and Bishop Spotels to move on by the earliest flight they could get.

He told them the English crowd were fickle, and hadn't forgiven their countrymen for beating England at the Ashes. They took the hint, and Thomas, now nearly recovered – with his head bandaged and a pad over one eye – hustled them away through the back door, and drove them to the airport.

He promised to send apologies to his own bishop, as soon as he was able to visit him in intensive care. Thomas, silently, also made it perfectly clear what he thought of the foreign visitors from the antipodes; they were barbarians.

He dumped the luggage on the ground, nodded to the guests, jumped into the car, and drove away at speed. The cardinal muttered irritably to Sammy something about 'curry-eaters, what could you expect?'

An hour later, there were in the air and Sammy, settling himself in his economy seat with resignation, found himself slowly adjusting to the situation, and began to smile secretly. It struck him as in keeping with the past fifteen years of his life, that, although they had travelled nearly 12,000 miles, they had encountered another situation that was just the same as would have happened – one way or another – had they stayed at home.

Well, he hadn't seen much of England; that was for sure. He had been hoping for a *glimpse* of England and that's exactly what he got – a glimpse! Ah well, he settled himself philosophically, a glimpse was better than none at all. Roll on Rome, and then home! Blessed home!

***

Six weeks later, a very tired cardinal, and a weary bishop, were glad to be back in familiar surroundings. The previous weeks had been exhausting: with intensive, endless working meetings for Sammy, and many, many, boring reunions with fellow cardinals, for Charles. However, back home again, both cardinal and bishop had to face the fact that their days together were numbered. They had only one month left for frantic preparations, and then Sammy would be gone.

At last the packing was done, and the day had arrived. The cardinal had insisted on going to the airport with Bishop Spotels. Sammy was not sure this was a good idea. However, there was no dissuading the cardinal, so both men travelled, utterly silent, in a car driven by Mrs Luigi Costello.

It didn't help either of the two men, having Amy Costello wiping away tears with a tissue, only one hand on the steering wheel of the car, and snuffling dreadfully.

At the airport, Sammy, juggling his hand luggage, was finally ready to enter the departure lounge. He offered his hand to Amy who burst out crying, gave him a big hug, then ran away, weeping loudly. Keeping his face utterly blank, Sammy asked:

"Do you think, Eminence, you'll be able to behave yourself – in a manner befitting a prince of the church – now that *I'm* not here to keep you *under tight control?"*

The cardinal, who had been on the brink of tears, reacted with spirit. He replied tartly: "That'll be the day, my lord Bishop! *You control me?* All these years I've had to put up with you and your damn, smelly motorbike, and your running, and your push-ups and skip-roping … and as for your singing … well … let me tell you, words fail me …"

"Well, thanks be to God for that! The number of times I've had to put up with your interminable sermons … they went on and on, and on; so many times all I wanted to do was to duck out, and have a cup of coffee. They were enough to make me wonder about taking up smoking … Why, I remember …"

The disembodied voice of the loud speaker announced: "The plane leaving for Algeria via … …"

Both men stopped their clowning. Sammy knelt immediately on the cement floor of the terminal, and spoke quietly. "Eminence, please bless me … and then, *please* just go …and … *thank you … for the happiest years of my life."*

The cardinal blessed the kneeling man with trembling hands quickly, and pulled him to his feet. He then took the younger man in his arms, and said brokenly, "Oh, Sammy! … Sammy! … …"

Bishop Spotels broke away, patted the cardinal's shoulder gently, and picking up his belongings, turned and went through the door, not trusting himself to look back. Charles stood still, unheedful of the tears pouring down his cheeks.

Amy returned, and silently taking his hand, led the old man quietly back to the car.

ARABIAN FRIGHTS

I was a fool to accept the invitation, Charles Cardinal York muttered irritably, as he swayed precariously on a camel's back. He had never ridden a camel before, and determined – if he could possibly help it – never to ride one ever again. He wondered, as he swished numerous flies from his sweating face, if that new bronchitis mixture that the doctor had given him, could be used as an embrocation – his hind quarters were killing him!

"How much longer?" he queried of the guide, Ibrahim

"Longer? What is mean, longer? I no know, longer."

"Farther to travel, you id … er … um … my … good man."

"I not your *good* man; I very *bad* man: I rob … I cheat … sometime I kill."

Good God! I've been given a murderer as a guide, the cardinal shuddered. Sammy will pay for this – he made all the travel arrangements!

However … as he was stuck with this wild character now, it might be prudent to try to placate this barbaric native son of the desert. The cardinal's opinion of the guide was that he looked so authentically evil, that he could easily have come straight from Central Casting.

With a renewed awareness of his precarious position, the cardinal tried a conciliatory tone.

"Ibrahim, your city, Darumbuljka – it is a big city, yes? I'm looking forward to visiting it." Charles knew, even as he said it, that that was simply *not* true.

After three days on a camel's back, he just wanted to be back home, safe and sound, in the Cathedral city he had foolishly left for this ridiculously sentimental journey, to visit his one-time secretary – now the Bishop of the See of Darumbuljka.

The guide seemed flattered by interest in his home town. He actually spoke quietly – for a change – to his elderly charge; his long flowing clothes and his head covering, moving dramatically, as he described his city.

"Sir, Darumbuljka … most beautiful city in desert. Here when Nabataeans rule Petra. They build my city; is called 'brown' city of plains – Petra be 'red' city."

"Really? How interesting. Are there very big buildings there – you know – with tall … you know … um … *high* buildings?"

"Yes, effendi, there are two buildings which are sky-touchers."

"Sky-*touchers*? What on *earth*? Oh, yes, I *do* see what you mean," the cardinal decided to change the subject.

"Do you know the holy Abuna, the Bishop Samuel Spotels?"

"Oh yes," grinned Ibrahim, showing his teeth – hidden before by his beard. "Everyone him knows. Great fighter, the Abuna!" He laughed aloud, letting go the leading rein of the camel – to the terror of the cardinal – and pranced around imitating a prize fighter, clothes flowing in every direction. The old man watched the performance in horror:

Dear God, he worried, what on earth has Sammy been doing? What does this hairy fellow mean, a 'great fighter'? Has the heat of the desert and the isolation turned Sammy's head?

Well, I'll just have to wait and see; perhaps I can do something about the situation, but I must try to remember that he's *not* just an auxiliary Bishop now; and he's definitely not just the young secretary I once had, all those years ago. He may not welcome any interference from me. But ... *fighting*! That didn't bode well for the dignity of the Episcopacy.

The cardinal's thoughts were interrupted by his guide pulling the camels to a halt.

"What's the matter, Ibrahim? Are we there yet? All I can see are a couple of tents near that sand-dune. Is this Darumbuljka? It surely can't be ... *can* it?"

The heavily bearded guide laughed loudly, and adjusted the long knife at his belt, flourishing it wildly. The huge blade caught the blood red rays of the setting sun and gleamed wickedly. The cardinal averted his eyes and began to pray audibly.

After fixing his knife to his satisfaction in his sash, the guide answered:

"No, not Darumbuljka! That funny! This very beautiful, very modern, very hygienic, wash-up, bath-up, clean-up, dress-up, station. You like very much. Get down now, careful ... camel kneel down ... Ooops! You *slide* off; I tell you many times ... No worry ... sand soft."

The cardinal picked himself up carefully from the sand, and followed the guide with apprehension into the first of the tents. To his alarm he was seized by two burly men, naked to the waist with their heads in turbans.

In total silence, his clothing was removed, and he closed his eyes thinking his time had come, but hastily opened them as he was physically lifted and placed in a steaming bath.

The men left him alone – to his intense relief – to scrub himself clean. After bathing, he stood waiting for his clothes and found that a complete new outfit was brought in to him.

To his stunned amazement, it was full Episcopal dress, complete with a beautiful mitre studded with gems. There was even a crosier of the finest silver. He dressed slowly and looked, bewildered, at the beautiful vestments he was now wearing. None of this made sense!

In a state of wonder he was led to a camel – a different one – magnificently caparisoned, and when mounted, he sat tall and stately, his crosier in his left hand.

"Little way go, now," chattered Ibrahim happily, "just round dunghill."

As they rounded the hill, Charles gasped in wonder. Before him was a great city, very modern, cable television dishes visible on the houses, streets well paved; the place buzzing with life, and sparklingly clean!

He was confused – he had been expecting a few mud hovels and great squalor. To add to his confusion, the Mosque, large and imposing as he expected it would be, was apparently ringing what sounded like, of all things, the *Angelus*!

The cardinal wondered if it were *he*, perhaps, who was suffering from heat stroke; he was imagining things. However, he was relieved to discover that a huge cathedral was situated very near the Mosque, and it was from *there* that the bells rang out gloriously.

As the news of his arrival spread, the main street was filling with people, including a number of nuns, who joined the populace in clapping and cheering their welcome to their distinguished visitor. With a tremendous effort, the cardinal pulled himself together and began to give a series of blessings as he processed along the street towards the cathedral.

There was a party waiting to welcome the cardinal, and Charles saw, to his amazement, that the Iman was there waiting alongside Bishop Samuel Spotels on the dismounting block.

Even more surprising, was the sight of a *boxing ring* erected directly outside the main steps of the cathedral!

Bishop Spotels helped the cardinal to alight, and for a moment held the old man tenderly in his arms. As he hugged the cardinal, Sammy whispered to Charles: "Be polite to the Iman won't you? I beat him at chess the other night, so he had to agree with our bells ringing the Angelus for one week – nice bloke really, educated at Oxford, fearfully clever, and a keen boxer as well. Now for the speeches." He released the cardinal.

Bishop Spotels, speaking surprisingly well in Arabic, welcomed the distinguished visitor with sincere gratitude for making the long and difficult journey; then the Iman welcomed Charles on behalf of the city

Charles in his turn, having no Arabic, spoke in English thanking his hosts for the wonderful welcome and expressing his awe at the beauty of their city.

It was a typical, 'response to a welcome' talk that the cardinal had had to give on many an occasion, and he wondered – as Bishop Sammy Spotels translated what he said – why the people shrieked with laugher – it wasn't meant to be funny!

Eventually, they adjourned inside the bishop's house – the Iman excusing himself – and Charles and Sammy were alone at last. Gratefully Charles removed the mitre from his head, and sipped the ice-cold lemonade he was given with real pleasure.

"Are we *really* alone, my Lord Bishop," he asked between sips.

"We certainly are, Eminence," Sammy replied, "it's just like old times."

"Well, not quite," responded the cardinal. "A couple of questions, Sammy. Firstly, what is the purpose of that boxing ring outside the cathedral?" Sammy's eyes began to twinkle with mischief. If the cardinal had been less fatigued, he would have recognized the signs at once: the bishop was going to trick him again!

"Simple really, Eminence. Whenever there is a religious difference between two of the Christians, in order to stop it getting out of hand, I put them in the ring and the winner after three rounds, is in the right! *He* has the correct theology."

"Wha-a-a-t!" spluttered the Cardinal.

"And, when the Iman – his name is Feisal – has a similar problem with his flock, he puts them in the same ring under the same rules."

"But, isn't there a court of higher appeal?"

"Oh course there is! We're not barbarians here! If there's still trouble – even after the fight in the ring – then the winner has to take on either me or the Iman. If they can beat us, then they are the winners, but, as we're both champs in the ring, so far no one has taken us on. Simple really."

"Sammy, I have to tell you this is not right; you will have to change all that; we'll have to discuss it later, but first, tell me why did the people laugh so much at what I said?"

Bishop Spotels looked a little embarrassed.

"Well, Eminence, I sort of … *spiced* up your speech a bit – you know, made it a bit more crowd-pleasing …"

"In what way?"

"Well, I said you were telling them, for their own good, that you were the retired middle-weight wrestling champion in the Western World and that, if they didn't behave, you'll take on, personally, any man over the age of eighty-two."

"You *what*? Are you out of your mind? … No, don't attempt to explain anything more to me Sammy. I cannot take any more today; I'm going to bed." As the cardinal stood up, he happened to glance out of the window.

His eyes goggled as he saw a small helicopter parked outside in the side garden.

"Whose helicopter is that?" he demanded sharply, suspicion rising in his mind.

"Why, mine of course; you don't think I go traipsing around

on *camels* when I want to visit my Diocese, do you?"

"Why … you … you … wretched man! You made me ride that flea-infested animal for three days in the scorching sun, and through that ghastly sand …"

"Well, I knew you thought this place was right out of the pages of the Arabian Nights, so I thought I give you a little glimpse of the romance of the desert – you know, the camels, the dust storms, the tents, the scorpions, the fleas, the lions that still roam the area – real movie sort of stuff. Now, you wouldn't want to miss that, would you?"

Sammy had to dodge as Charles threw all the cushions in the room at his erstwhile secretary. Having exhausted the supply, he reached for the lamp stand before suddenly deciding he'd had enough. He demanded to be taken to his room – it had been a long and very confusing day.

However, on reaching his room, the cardinal found that the confusion had not yet ended. Lying on his bed was a very large metal key attached to a big bow of red ribbon. A printed note lay under the key. It read:

Use this key and open your eyes

Look up and you'll get a big surprise.

The cardinal looked at the note, puzzled. The doggerel was so bad, it had to be from Sammy, but what did it mean? He shrugged; he was too tired for anything else tonight. But tomorrow! He would solve the mystery then.

***

Cardinal, Charles York was a very old man yet he still rose from bed before six in the mornings. When he had retired to a home for elderly clerics, he continued the practice of a lifetime, and was always in the chapel for Mass, forty-five minutes later. This morning was no different in spite of the fatigues of the past days, and the strangeness of his surroundings.

When he entered the cathedral he was surprised to see that Bishop Sammy Spotels was just leaving; his Mass already finished. Goodness, he thought, this is very impressive; Sammy – in spite of the boxing ring and everything else – seems to be doing a good job. Charles, left alone with the master of ceremonies, stared, puzzled at the man – there was something familiar about him … Suddenly he realised what it was!

"Ibrahim! What are you doing here? You've shaved off your beard, you villain. Don't tell me you're actually a *Christian*."

"Oh course, I am, Your Eminence," Ibrahim replied in his beautiful English educated voice, "We have been for centuries." The young man came and knelt at Charles' feet.

"Eminence, I humbly beg pardon for the deception I played on you during your journey. His Lordship, Bishop Spotels asked me to do it as a special favour."

"You mean you were only pretending not to be able to speak English?"

"Of course, Eminence. I was educated in England – Harrow actually – then went on to Cambridge."

The cardinal was bewildered. "Then, why on earth, after that, did you come back *here*?"

As soon as the words were out of his mouth, Charles realised how rude they would have sounded, so hastened to soften what he had implied: "I mean, it's a lovely city, no doubt about that, but after London …"

"Too many foreigners there, Eminence; you know, *dark* people! My family decided to return, and I agreed with them. I work at the University here."

"And you are Bishop Spotels' master of ceremonies?"

"Indeed I am, and my brother is an expert in Gregorian Chant;

he will lead the choir today."

The cardinal sat down abruptly in the only chair in the vestry. He spoke slowly:

"Ibrahim, I think I've managed so far to get everything wrong. I think it might be wise if you helped me to dress now for Mass."

***

After breakfast, Sammy explained that he had to be out for a couple of hours, so excused himself and left the cardinal alone – to his relief. Now, he could try to solve the mystery of the key. He waited impatiently until he heard the door slam after Sammy, then prepared to act.

The cardinal took the key from his pocket and studied it carefully. It was beautifully made, about six inches long. Keeping a lookout for any servants, or any other people, in the house, he began trying the key in every door lock he could find. It fitted none of them.

As he neared the rear of the large building, Charles found himself outside the kitchen door, and saw to his astonishment, that there was another building directly behind the bishop's house. It had a big and very impressive door. Charles felt sure he had found the solution to the mystery.

He advanced on the door, inserted the key and gave a loud whoop, as the door swung open.

His mouth dropped open when he found Sammy standing there grinning.

"Welcome home, Eminence," he said, "this is your new home."

"My what? Is this another of your crazy games?"

"Go outside again, Eminence, and look up over the door." The cardinal did so and clutched the door post for support. Over the lintel was his very own crest and coat of arms.

"But I don't understand, Sammy ..."

"Look Eminence, you have retired. You have no family left, so I thought, why not come here to me? I've had this place specially built for you; there's a study with the internet connected, your own phone, two bedrooms – in case you would like to invite a friend to stay – your own kitchen, but you'll be having your meals with me, of course, unless you want to do things yourself. There's a good sitting room and, best of all, Eminence, it's all air-conditioned."

"Sammy, could I please come in and sit down." The old cardinal came shakily into the house, and sat in one of the comfortable armchairs. He looked at his one-time secretary.

"Sammy, why are you doing this for me? It's unheard of ... it's also the nicest thing anyone has ever done for me in my whole life."

Sammy was embarrassed. "Well, we always got on rather well, didn't we? And, to tell the truth, I've missed you." Sammy gave a cheeky grin. "I especially missed all those dreadful things you did – getting me mixed up with the police and everything ... the truth is, everything is pretty tame out here without you."

The cardinal was deeply touched. He dreaded that he might actually burst into tears at any moment, "So, you built this for ... me ..."

"Yes, it's called a 'Granny Flat,' so, of course once you're in residence I'll call you 'Granny' and ..."

"You'll *WHAT*? Over my dead body!"

Sammy went on. "And, as you're so obviously over the hill, you'll not be able to play tricks on me anymore." Sammy dodged a glass bowl that missed his head by inches. He slipped out the door, popping his head back in to say quickly: "And, poor old chap, now just ready to sit in the old rocking chair ..." As another missile crashed against the door, Sammy retreated laughing.

Back in his new home, the cardinal chuckled. This is going to be fun, he thought. And there I was, thinking I'd be sitting in the retirement village, sharing endless boring stories with other old blokes. Whereas here! Well, if Sammy thinks the 'old boy' is finished playing jokes, he's got another think coming.

His thoughts were interrupted by a knocking at the door. Sammy's head popped in again. "I say, there's a special camel race on; I know you wouldn't be interested – it's a young man's sport – but I'm going to have a bet on the race, so, see you later…"

The cardinal jumped up quickly.

"Wait for me," he shouted, "you cheeky fellow, I'm coming."

Sammy chuckled happily, as he turned to leave; *things were already back to normal!*

BACKGROUND TO THIS BOOK

It is difficult for most people to realise that VIPs live two separate lives; one the exterior image they present, and are expected to present, to the public, and the private and inner being that exists behind the social mask.

Since man existed on the earth those who held important secular or religious roles have worn special clothing of one sort or another, and were expected to act, speak, behave, and above all, to be models of behaviour of whatever kind that was valued highly by the society in which they functioned. Mankind was aware that to remove those exterior 'trappings' would risk demeaning the office held, so that it would soon become totally socially and morally irrelevant.

George Eliot, one of the greatest of the masters of English Literature, had this in mind when she wrote: 'Scenes of Clerical Life.' She wanted to highlight the *human being*, inside the public figure. Without conscious thought of Eliot, I think that is what encouraged me to create these two characters: the Cardinal and the Secretary/MC.

I created these two men from two real characters I had known. I knew the Cardinal personally and was aware of his shining innocence which was coupled to a fiendish sense of humour; I was aware of how difficult it was for him to be always dignified, solemn, calm in the midst of horrendous problem situations, impeccably dressed – in fact all the things we, unconsciously, expect of the Sovereign, the grand old lady, herself.

With the secretary/MC it was easier, but he, too, could never say publicly what he thought privately. Sammy Spotels had to learn as he went on to play the role of a VIP, but as he was a super intelligent young man who had a very healthy outlet in his motor bike and his boxing, it was easier for him.

I think the best story in the group is the 'Class Reunion'. This is the one I entered in the US International Short Story Competition and, to my delight, was a runner-up prize winner. The editors said that the writing reminded them of Guareschi (The Little World of Don Camillo); I hope that is so.

In writing of my two characters and thinking of them for some years now, I've come to admire them and, as in the farewell scene between the two old friends at the airport, I think the genuine manly love that developed between the very old man and his young, faithful assistant is apparent – it is that of father and son. They are real human beings.

I've come to like my characters; I hope you do so too.

www.ingramcontent.com/pod-product-compliance
Lightning Source LLC
Chambersburg PA
CBHW021126130626
46554CB00002B/885